Jason swung he
around to face

"What's got into you
deny there's someth...

Mutely she met his eyes, accepting that
he spoke the truth, yet loath to
acknowledge the excitement he aroused
in her. Aware of it, he pulled her hard
against him.

"Stop," he ground out. "You're a woman
with normal, healthy desires, so why fight
them?"

It was the age-old cry of a man on the
make, and it angered her so much that
passion died and she found it easy to pull
away from him.

"I may have healthy desires, Jason, but I
don't think it healthy to give in to them
just because the mood takes me. So,
much as I fancy you, I won't go to bed
with you."

ROBERTA LEIGH wrote her first book at the age of nineteen and since then has written more than seventy romance novels, as well as many books and film series for children. She has also been an editor of a woman's magazine and produced a teen magazine, but writing romance fiction remains one of her greatest joys. She lives in Hampstead, London, and has one son.

Books by Roberta Leigh

Don't miss any of our special offers. Write to us at the following address for information on our newest releases.

Harlequin Reader Service
901 Fuhrmann Blvd., P.O. Box 1397, Buffalo, NY 14240
Canadian address: P.O. Box 603,
Fort Erie, Ont. L2A 5X3

ROBERTA LEIGH

a most unsuitable wife

Harlequin Books

TORONTO • NEW YORK • LONDON
AMSTERDAM • PARIS • SYDNEY • HAMBURG
STOCKHOLM • ATHENS • TOKYO • MILAN

Harlequin Presents first edition September 1990
ISBN 0-373-11298-X

Original hardcover edition published in 1989
by Mills & Boon Limited

CHAPTER ONE

THE GLEAMING grey Rolls glided to a stop, and the chauffeur jumped out swiftly and opened the back door. A tall, slender girl emerged, pulling her sable coat closer around her as she shivered in the cold wind. The glossy fur was as silky as her long, honey-blonde hair. Only her wide-set hazel eyes and high cheekbones were visible as she lifted the collar higher and glided away from the car, setting one high-heeled foot gracefully in front of the other.

'Cut!' shouted a stentorian voice. 'Take ten minutes.'

The cameras whirred to a stop, the wind machine was stilled, and the girl grinned at the 'chauffeur' and went across the pavement to where Bud Weston, the director, was standing.

'How was it?' Lorraine Ellis asked.

'Great. But we'll do it once more as insurance!'

She chuckled, for Bud—whose TV commercials had won him many awards—was a perfectionist. Repeating this scene would be a terrible sweat—literally—for the current temperature was twenty-eight degrees. Yet it was no worse than shivering in summer dresses while Siberian winds whipped round her!

'I'm ready when you are,' she said aloud.

'I only wish you meant it,' he joked.

She chuckled again, her perfectly contoured mouth curving upwards, her eyes lightening so one saw the paler yellow flecks in them. 'Circe's eyes,' a disgruntled suitor had once called them, 'promising everything and giving nothing.' But better that, she had decided, than relationships where commitment was neither considered nor required.

'OK!' Bud ordered. 'Let's go for a final take.'

As Lorraine returned to the car, the assistant director darted over to her with a slip of paper.

'Your answering service called in with an urgent message for you to telephone Denis Brampton in London. Here's the number.'

Wondering why her brother's best friend had called her, she stuffed the paper into the pocket of her coat and slid into the car, anxious for the filming to be over.

It was half an hour before she was able to contact Denis from the mobile van which doubled as dressing-room and office. What he had to say drained the light from her eyes, and she crumpled on to a nearby chair, unable to believe her brother and sister-in-law had been killed in a car accident that morning, leaving four-year-old Jilly and eight-year-old Paul orphans.

Why had a loving deity destroyed such a happy family? she wondered bitterly. And they *had* been happy, despite the gloomy forecasts of Lord and Lady Stanway, Anne's unbending parents, who had refused to acknowledge her existence after her marriage.

'How dare they look down on you?' Lorraine had ranted to her brother when he had told her. He was ten years her senior, and from the time she was eleven—when their parents had died—he had taken care of her.

'It isn't a matter of looking down,' Edward had replied. 'They simply think Anne isn't looking up!

And I can appreciate their point. After all, a struggling actor is hardly the son-in-law they've envisaged!'

Even after Paul's birth, when Edward was already making a name for himself, Anne's parents had not relented, and recalling this Lorraine accepted that Paul and Jilly were now her responsibility. It was a tough burden, but she would shoulder it with love.

At eight o'clock that evening she boarded a flight to London, and was met at Heathrow by Denis Brampton. His wife Sally had been at drama school with Edward, and had soon become Anne's closest friend.

'Sally's with Paul and Jilly,' Denis explained, his eyes misty as he gave her a bear-hug. 'We didn't think it wise to bring them with us to meet you.'

'Thanks. I need time to pull myself together.'

Yet nothing could stem her tears as the two children rushed down the garden path to greet her as she stepped from the car, Jilly's short, chubby legs matching Paul's longer, knobbly-kneed ones, so that they both collapsed against her simultaneously, almost knocking her over as she bent and spread her arms wide to enfold them.

It was equally painful to enter the pretty little house and find no Edward or Anne to greet her. But she pushed the thought aside and allowed the children to take her upstairs to the yellow and white spare room that was hers when she paid them a visit.

'I'm responsible for the children now,' she repeated later in the day to Sally and Denis. 'Are there any legalities I must go through before I take them with me to the States? I'd like to leave as soon after the funeral as possible.'

'Is that wise?' Sally ventured. 'I'm no psychologist, but I think such a sudden upheaval will add to their distress.'

'So do I,' Denis concurred, his freckled face earnest. 'Can't you give them a chance to come to terms with their parents' death before uprooting them?'

'I thought it better to make a fresh start as quickly as possible,' Lorraine answered. 'But if you think it will distress them, I'll stay on here a few months longer. Luckily I've a healthy bank balance and can afford a break.'

'There's no need to delay *your* return,' Sally said. 'Denis and I will be happy to have the children for the summer, and it will give you a chance to organise things.'

Though it was an excellent suggestion, Lorraine didn't fancy leaving Jilly and Paul for even a few months. An image of Edward as she had last seen him—tall, blond and smiling—rose before her, and her resolve to remain with the children solidified.

'I've worked flat out in New York,' she stated, 'and after four years I deserve a rest.'

'Some rest, taking care of two kids,' Sally said drily.

'You won't need to use your savings,' Denis intervened. 'I was Edward's lawyer, as you're aware, and he did very well these last few years. He also had a decent insurance policy which will pay for the children's education.'

'That's a relief,' Lorraine admitted.

'One other thing. Edward was quite well-known, and the car crash made a lot of coverage, so you'd better brace yourself to see Anne's parents at the funeral.'

He was right, for the angular figure of Lord Stanway and the smaller, plumper one of his wife—Lorraine recognised them from a photograph Anne had once shown her—were the first she spotted at the cemetery three days later. Anxious to avoid them, she hurried towards Denis's car the moment the service was over, but escape was impossible, for they caught up with her.

'Miss Ellis, I wish to speak with you.' Lord Stanway's voice, though thin, was autocratic, and his cavernous eyes moved slowly over her. 'I want you to know you won't have to concern yourself with the children's welfare. They will make their home with us.'

'That won't be necessary,' Lorraine said stiffly. 'Their father left them adequately provided for, and they'll be living with me in New York.'

'They are English and should remain in their own country.'

'They will be brought up by someone they know and love,' Lorraine couldn't resist saying. 'You and your wife are strangers to them. It's how you wanted it, and now you're reaping the reward of your actions.'

'Please don't judge us, Miss Ellis,' Lady Stanway intervened in a shaky voice. 'We have as much right to the children as you.'

Lorraine felt a momentary pang as she stared into the red-rimmed eyes of Anne's mother. Edward had maintained that it was his father-in-law who had opposed the marriage, and that his wife had been obliged to go along with him. Now Paul and Jilly were the woman's only link with the daughter she had lost.

'I'm sorry, Lady Stanway, but the children will be living with *me*.'

'We'll fight for them,' Lord Stanway barked, eyeing her beautifully cut black suit and careful make-up. 'I can't imagine you giving up your career to take care of them. From the look of you, modelling's the be-all of your life.'

'Henry!' his wife remonstrated. 'We all mask our grief differently.'

'A painted face and high fashion isn't in the best of taste for a funeral,' he persisted.

Lorraine swung round and ran to the car, devastated that her appearance had been misjudged. She had made an effort to look her best, for the children loved it when she dressed up, and Edward too would have wanted her to show a brave face in the world.

'Made a scene, did they?' Denis murmured as she slipped into the car beside him.

She nodded, giving him the gist of it as they drove off.

'You haven't heard the last of them,' he warned. 'They have the money to fight you.'

'Their claim isn't greater than mine.'

'I'm not so sure. But they'll certainly have the children made wards of court until a judge decides their future.'

'Which means?'

'They can't leave the country until a ruling's been given.'

A few days later Lord Stanway did exactly that, and Lorraine exploded into Denis's office, waving the document delivered to her that morning.

'I'll fight him in every court in the country!' she stormed.

'You may lose,' Denis warned. 'Unfortunately Edward didn't make you the children's legal guardian.'

'There must be *something* we can do. As far as Paul and Jilly are concerned, I'm their only family!'

'The Stanways will argue that the children are young enough to form other attachments, and that they can also give them every material advantage, as well as bring them up in their own country. The last bit counts for a lot.'

'If necessary, I'll come back here to live,' Lorraine asserted. 'And you can inform the Stanways that I'll tell the world how shabbily they treated their only child, and how, the moment she's dead, they can't wait to get their hands on two grandchildren they've always refused to recognise!'

'Don't make threats,' cautioned Denis. 'You'll do better with the courts by being gentle. If I find we're getting nowhere, *then* we'll don boxing gloves.'

Lorraine stared intently into Denis's serious, kindly face. 'I'll hold you to it,' she said flatly, and, five feet eight of fighting woman, stalked from the room.

CHAPTER TWO

'SUPPER, come and get it!' Lorraine called, barely hearing herself above the din from the living-room.

'What on earth are you two doing in there?' she called in exasperation, wiping her hands on her food-spattered apron. 'Oh, lord, who can that be?' she muttered as the bell rang, and she dashed into the hall to open the door.

As she did, two miniature Red Indians came whooping out of the living-room and bounded to-wards her and the man on the doorstep, their red and white painted faces grotesque in the shad-owy passage.

'Be quiet, both of you!' she shouted above their war-whoops, but they took no notice and rushed up-stairs, the noise receding as the bedroom door banged shut behind them.

'Sorry about that,' she apologised, turning to the stranger.

'Quite a welcome!' Teeth flashed white in a tanned face, and Lorraine was suddenly aware of her un-kempt appearance. Automatically she smoothed back her hair, looping a long honey-gold strand behind her ear.

'Now you've streaked cream on it,' he said.

'On what?'

'Your hair.'

Dark grey eyes, betraying a hint of humour, met hers, and she blushed like a schoolgirl, raised her hand

to remove the cream, then thought better of it. She'd
wait till she was in front of a mirror.

'Forget my hair,' she mumbled. 'What do you
want?'

'Firstly that you put a safety chain on the front
door before opening it.' He took a step forward and
was in the hall beside her. 'You don't know me from
Adam,' he went on, his well-shaped mouth curling
grimly, 'yet you fling open the door and let me into
your home.'

Lorraine panicked momentarily, but then the man
smiled, and she relaxed.

'I'm serious,' he said. 'It's dangerous to allow
strangers into your home, and you should warn your
children not to talk to them either.'

She flushed at the reprimand. 'I'm sure you didn't
ring the bell to tell me this.'

'I didn't. I none the less think it advisable to say
it.'

As her eyes grew accustomed to the dim evening
light, she saw him clearly. What a stunner he was!
His strong, even-featured face, with its glinting grey
eyes, straight nose and sensuous mouth, was well-
matched by a wide-shouldered, slim-hipped body. He
was tall too, topping her own five foot eight by at
least six inches. She felt very small beside him; an
unusual occurrence she enjoyed.

'I've come to see Mr Edward Ellis,' he announced.

Lorraine felt as if she'd been hit in the stomach,
this simple request reminding her that she would never
see her brother again.

'I—I'm afraid he—my brother and his wife were
killed in a car crash.' Her eyes flooded with tears and
she half turned away.

'I'm terribly sorry—I'd no idea,' the man apologised. 'I've recently returned from Australia and a friend out there asked me to look him up.'

'You must mean James,' she said. 'He was in rep with Edward and went to Australia to do a TV series.'

'It wasn't James,' the man said. 'It was a chap called Lawrence.'

'Well, never mind.' She moved back a step. 'Please stay and have a drink. And excuse my appearance. I was preparing the children's supper.'

Without comment, he followed her into the living-room.

'Are you an actor too?' she asked, pouring him a glass of wine, then perching on the edge of an armchair while he sank into the one across from her.

'No, I write. Jason Fletcher's the name.'

'Espionage thrillers!'

He grinned. 'On the nail!'

Her eyes took in every detail of him: the well-cut grey suit and Gucci shoes, the gold Rolex on the strong wrist, the bronzed face and the thick black hair lying sleek over a well-shaped head. Aware of his gaze roaming the room, she rose to collect the stray toys, books and colouring pencils scattered on the floor.

'Excuse the mess,' she apologised. 'These past few weeks I've let the children do as they like.'

'Don't tidy up on my account.'

'I do in the evenings, anyway.'

He reached for a crumpled newspaper and handed it to her. 'You don't look like a *Times* reader!' he observed drily.

He had a point, she reflected, conscious of her soiled apron, scruffy jeans and crumpled T-shirt. In her anguish she had only brought a few clothes with her from New York, and knew what an unprepossessing sight she was.

'No offence meant,' he added quickly. 'Caring for two youngsters can't be easy.'

As if on cue, Paul and Jilly came bounding in, smothered in perfumed talc which sent up a fine white cloud around them.

'For heaven's sake!' Lorraine exclaimed, and Jason Fletcher hurriedly jumped to his feet and tried to dust off the white coating which had settled on his suit.

'You're making it worse,' she warned, deeply embarrassed. 'If you wait while I find a brush——' Suddenly the humour of the situation struck her, and she chuckled.

'I'm glad you find it funny,' he grunted.

Instantly she sobered. 'I'm not used to domesticity,' she confessed.

'I hope you soon learn—for the children's sake.'

'You're very concerned for them,' she said acidly.

'With good cause. You let me walk into the house and——'

'That was careless, I admit, but——'

'It only needs one careless action and you could all be murdered!'

'Stop being melodramatic,' she said crossly. 'You're a complete stranger and you've no business lecturing me.'

His reply was cut short by Jilly running over and hugging her. 'Don't be upset, Lorri.'

'I'm not, darling.' Lorraine cuddled her niece close and, straightening, saw the man watching her with an inscrutable expression. 'Apologise to our visitor for getting powder all over him,' she prompted.

Jilly stared at him but said nothing, then silently joined her brother, who was scribbling on a piece of paper on the floor.

'They've been through a traumatic time,' Lorraine explained. 'That's why I go easy on them.'

'That's no reason for you not to be firm. Children regard it as a kind of security.'

'You're very *au fait* about children, Mr Fletcher. Do you have——?'

'Something's burning!' he shouted, and in a flash was out of the room and into the kitchen. Dense smoke was pouring from it as Lorraine and the children followed him in.

'Keep out!' he ordered angrily, dumping a smoking pan of oil into the sink.

'Will the house burn down?' Jilly called anxiously.

'Of course not,' Lorraine comforted. 'It's only the fish fryer.'

'Only?' the man snarled, eyes streaming. 'If I hadn't been here, it might well have been the whole house!'

'If you hadn't been here and I hadn't been talking to you, I wouldn't have forgotten I'd put it on to heat.'

'How could you forget a pan of oil?' Thick black brows rose skywards. 'There aren't two children in this house—there are three!' His eyes lighted on another pan, its interior filled with charred black remains. 'What's this, for pity's sake?'

'Spinach,' she confessed, stretching out a hand to lift the smouldering pan from the cooker.

'Watch out, it's hot!' he warned.

But it was too late, and with a yelp she dropped the pan on the cooker, pain searing her fingers.

He swore beneath his breath. 'Where's your first-aid box?'

'We don't have one.'

'Ice, then?'

Not waiting for her answer, he turned on the cold water and put her hand under it, then took a few ice-cubes from the refrigerator. Placing them in a snow-white handkerchief, he bound it round her fingers. Even through her pain she noticed how beautifully shaped his hands were, and the fine black hairs on his wrist.

'I guess I'm an all-round failure,' she muttered, shock and pain bringing her close to tears.

'Now who's being melodramatic?' he chided. His eyes rested on her clearly defined breasts, bra-less beneath her T-shirt, then flicked down to the slim curve of her hips encased in tight jeans. 'I'm sure you'll soon learn.'

'I hope so,' she said fervently. 'But it's all so new to me. I'm a model in New York,' she added, 'and I live in a modern apartment with a jewel of a daily.'

'No wonder you find this hard,' Jason Fletcher said drily.

'I'se hungry,' Jilly piped up.

'Me too,' Paul added. 'I can eat a horse.'

'No horses today!' Lorraine grinned, and opened a cupboard just above her. As assortment of tinned food, baked beans, spaghetti and soups, tumbled out, and the children shrieked with laughter.

'Not exactly cordon bleu,' she said to Jason Fletcher, airily waving a can of ravioli, 'but better than burnt spinach!'

For an instant his features were rigid, then his mouth quirked, his frown dissolved and he chuckled. What a change in him! The dark grey eyes lightened, the line of his mouth softened sensuously, and his air of hauteur vanished. At first sight she had considered him handsome—at second, fabulous.

'I really do apologise for the mess,' she reiterated, waving a bandaged hand around the kitchen. 'I'll feed the children, then clear up.'

'I'll help you.'

'Absolutely not. I *do* know how to use a brush and pan!'

'Ever modelled with one?' he drawled, and she laughed and shook her head.

'I do glamour products—furs, jewellery, make-up. Though I dare say you find it hard to believe,' she added self-consciously.

'Not at all. You're doing a great job for the new range of mascara you're plugging!' Delicately he ran his finger under her eye, then showed her the black soot on the tip of it. 'It might be better if you stuck to modelling and let your nephew and niece be brought up by someone trained for it.'

'There's only me,' she said coldly, her anger returning at his criticism.

'You mean they've no other relatives?'

'No one loves them as much as I do,' she stated firmly, 'and love is what they need most.'

'Love and canned ravioli,' came the sardonic comment.

'Which is a darn sight better than fillet steak and no love!' she snapped.

'True.'

With a mocking wave he was gone, and she slammed down the can on the table. How dared a complete stranger walk in and set himself up as her judge and jury?

Yet he hadn't been totally wrong, she reflected later in the evening, when she had tucked Paul and Jilly into bed and crawled wearily into the living-room. She'd rather do ten modelling sessions than one day of this! But once they were in the States she would organise things differently. She'd have to, or she wouldn't be free to continue her career.

And it was important she did, for in the next four or five years she had to earn as much as possible, before younger models ousted her from the top earning bracket. What would she do with her life then? It was a worrying thought, but she pushed it aside. First things first. And the next step was to prepare the children for their move to the States.

Yawning, she turned off the lights and went into the hall to check that the front door was locked. As she did, she thought of Jason Fletcher.

He really was a strange man. Within moments of encountering her he had practically taken her over, dispensing first aid and advice with equal impartiality. A difficult husband to live up to, she mused, and wondered if he were married. He probably was. Handsome men whose talent also made them wealthy were unlikely to be single in their mid-thirties.

Upon which thought she sighed and went to bed.

More than ever determined to proved herself capable on the domestic front, Lorraine bought books on child care, cookery and housekeeping.

'You're too hard on yourself,' Sally had remarked when visiting her one afternoon to see how she was progressing. 'Learn to walk before you run.'

'I'd settle for being able to crawl! I'm hopeless, Sally.'

'Rubbish! The children are happy, aren't they? So who cares if the house is untidy and the food isn't gourmet?'

Lorraine hadn't answered, knowing she would sound a prize idiot if she admitted she wanted to look efficient in the eyes of a handsome male know-all she probably wouldn't see again!

But enough of Jason Fletcher, she thought now as she enjoyed a cup of coffee, grateful that Sally had taken Paul and Jilly to the zoo today, with her own brood.

A series of thumps outside brought her to the window. A removal van was parked in front of the next-door house, and the driver was unloading suitcases and boxes of books, one of which had crashed to the ground and strewn its contents on the pavement. Investigating was a tall, loose-limbed man, and her heart skipped a beat as she recognised Jason Fletcher. What was he doing here?

Seconds later she was out of the house and down the path, unmindful of her shiny face and untidy ponytail.

'Hi,' she called as she reached the gate.

He straightened and smiled. If anything, he was more devastating in broad daylight than at night, a picture of sartorial splendour in beige linen trousers and brown and beige open-necked shirt, the emblem of an Italian fashion house embroidered on the breast pocket.

'What are you dong here?' she asked.

'I'm moving in. When I visited you the other evening I noticed a "To Let" sign on this house, and as I've a book to finish and require a bolthole in which to do it, I decided to rent it.'

'Weren't you put off by having us as neighbours?' she joked.

'On the contrary, I'll be killing two birds with one stone. Finishing a book and keeping an eye on two orphans! And talking about keeping an eye, you've left your front door open again. The children might run into the street.'

'They're out for the day,' she said frigidly.

'Oops! I've put my foot in it again.'

The warm gleam in his eyes as they surveyed her neutralised her annoyance.

'If you'll excuse me,' he went on, bending to retrieve the few books still lying on the pavement, 'I've work to do.'

'Need help?' Lorraine asked tentatively.

'If you insist.' He smiled. 'But don't carry anything too heavy.'

'Do I look feeble?'

'No, but I don't see models as weight-lifters!'

She glared at him over the top of the pot plant she was carrying. 'We may look as though a breath of wind will blow us away, Mr Fletcher, but we have to be strong as oxen to stand up to some of our schedules. Try posing under arc lights for four hours in a photographer's studio, and then dash across the city to model fifteen different outfits in two hours for a bad-tempered couturier!'

'No offence meant,' he said hurriedly, 'I really am sorry.'

Magnanimously she carried the plant into the house.

'This place is beginning to look like home,' he pronounced an hour later, when the van had gone and he surveyed the few pieces of furniture he had brought with him: a leather-upholstered chair and teak desk, several lovely watercolours, and two shelves of books. 'Furnished lets are notoriously under-furnished, and I can't work unless the atmosphere is right.'

'I'm surprised you don't have your own place in London,' she said.

'I've an apartment in the Albany.'

It was a prestigious address and she was impressed. 'Then how come this?' She waved her arm around her.

'My friends won't know where to contact me. When I'm writing, I like to decide when I want to be distracted.'

She wasn't sure if he was diplomatically warning her to keep her distance, then decided he wasn't. After all, why should he when they barely knew each other?

'I'll leave you to it,' she murmured. 'Anything you need before I go?'

'No, thanks. I've stocked up the fridge and freezer.'

'How well-organised you are!'

'I've been taking care of myself since my twenties. What about you?' he went on. 'Do you live alone in New York?'

Regarding this as a not so subtle way of asking if she had a boyfriend, she said casually, 'Yes, but I eat out a lot.' She was at the door when he spoke again.

'Milk! That's the one thing I forgot.'

'No problem. I'll bring you some.'

She ran back home, returning sheepishly a few moments later. 'I'm sorry, but I've only enough for the children's breakfast.'

'Not to worry—I'll use Longlife. I keep a carton for emergencies.'

She had a feeling he was trying to show her how incompetent she was, then dismissed the idea as paranoid. 'Let me at least make you some coffee with it,' she contented herself with saying.

'Sounds great. But will you make it tea? And incidentally, the name's Jason.'

'Lorraine,' she responded with a smile, and disappeared into his kitchen, reappearing with two mugs of rather murky liquid.

'Odd colour,' he commented, his mouth twitching at the corners, as if trying not to smile.

'I couldn't find the kettle, so I boiled the water in a pot.'

'You didn't boil it long enough.'

'I'll make you another cup,' she offered.

'This will do,' he said politely. 'I'll just shut my eyes when I sip!'

Conscious of her inability to perform even the simplest household task, Lorraine gulped down her tea—which tasted perfectly fine to her—and left him to carry on with the rest of his unpacking.

The tribulations of housekeeping continued to nag at her in the days that followed, exacerbated by Jason popping in at unpredictable times, his visits invariably coinciding with Jilly and Paul at their worst.

But gradually she stopped worrying that neither she nor the house ever looked ready to receive visitors, and after his first few visits ceased apologising for it. If the untidiness and noise irritated him he could stay away. No, she didn't mean that. She enjoyed seeing him, and had become used to his gritty comments about her capabilities.

'You look exhausted,' he remarked one evening when he popped in to borrow a hammer.

'I am.' She half turned from the stove where she was grilling chops.

'Here's the hammer!' called Paul, brandishing it in the air.

'You'll hit someone, carrying it like that,' Lorraine warned, and in the nick of time grabbed it from him as Jilly raced in through the opposite door.

'Quick thinking,' Jason murmured, and Lorraine glowed. At last she had earned a compliment from him!

'Let *me* give the hammer to Jason!' Jilly's voice rose an octave as she tried to grab it from her brother.

Paul retaliated with a shove which sent her on to the floor, her shrieks resounding through the house.

'Poor darling!' Lorraine bent solicitously down to her, and was pulled back by Jason's hard grip.

'Cut it out, Jilly. You too, Paul.' His stentorian tone brought instant silence. 'Wash your hands, both of you, and sit at the table till dinner's ready.'

Meek as lambs, they did as ordered, and Lorraine gave Jason a grateful smile.

'I'm sorry I can't ask you to join me, but I've only grilled a couple of chops for the children. Oh!' She swung round to look at them, frightened they had burnt to a frazzle. Please, lord, not with Jason watching!

Sensing her agitation, he said hastily, 'I can't stay anyway, I'm dining out. But why don't I bring you one of my special Chinese dinners tomorrow evening, to save you cooking?'

'I like spare ribs,' Paul informed him.

'Me too,' Jilly endorsed.

'Me three,' added Lorraine, delighted by Jason's offer, though it had nothing to do with the food. 'Shall I make soup or a sweet?' she ventured.

'No, thanks, you deserve a night off.'

'Quick thinking, Fletcher!' she teased, and he chucked her under the chin as he left.

Next day she sped through the household chores, telling herself the bubbles of happiness inside had nothing to do with Jason, and knowing she was lying through her back teeth!

At midday she collected Jilly from play school and treated them both to lunch in a health bar, all the while cogitating on what to wear that evening. Fortunately some of her clothes had arrived from New York, and she veered between ultra-sophisticated or frothy and feminine. Still, she had all day to decide, though one thing was certain: a swan would emerge from her ugly duckling image to dazzle Jason Fletcher as he had never been dazzled before!

By six o'clock the children were in their pyjamas and enjoined—on pain of no supper—to watch television without messing up the living-room or themselves.

Only then did she allow herself to luxuriate in a bath of liberally scented water and contemplate the evening ahead. It was hard without recalling the tragic circumstances which had brought her here, and, resolutely blinking back the tears, she towelled herself briskly and set about transforming herself.

Her perfect skin needed no covering other than the merest touch of foundation, and she accentuated her high cheekbones with blusher, and her grey-green eyes with delicate almond green shadow. Only one coat of mascara was necessary for lashes already thick without it, and the merest touch of lip-gloss on a mouth that owed its wild rose colour to nature, not artifice.

Brushing her hair into golden silkiness, she coiled it into a chignon on the nape of her neck, pulling a

few tendrils loose at her temples. Then she reached
for the low-waisted Twenties-style dress she had finally decided on. The silvery grey silk lightly skimmed
her body and stopped at the knee, the material so fine
that, despite its loose cut, it clung subtly to every curve
of her tall, slender body. A long strand of shim-
mering pearls and drop ear-rings to match completed
the picture, and with the dispassion of a top model
she decided that if Jason wasn't bowled over by her
he had to be made of stone!

. She was in the living-room, rearranging a vase of
freesias, when he arrived. Paul let him in, sounding
very important as he did, and she hid a smile and left
him to it, the smile broadening as she heard him say,
'I 'spect you'll want to put the food in the oven. Lorri
put it on for you.'

'Great,' said Jason. 'Your aunt's really becoming
domesticated!'

I'll kill him! Lorraine fumed, then, smoothing her
dress across her hips, knew she could do much better.
Drawing a deep breath, she undulated into the kitchen
as Jason straightened from the oven.

Pole-axed, he stared at her, then swallowed hard.
'You're quite something!' he told her.

'Thank you,' she said graciously.

Jason was worth looking at too, resplendently
casual in Ralph Lauren trousers and a poplin shirt,
the sleeves rolled back to show muscular arms lightly
flecked with black hair. But she was mainly aware of
the strength he exuded. It was more than physical,
and came from an inner resource she had frequently
glimpsed.

'Care for a drink?' she asked.

He nodded and followed her into the living-room, but as she opened the sideboard to search out what was there he was beside her, a bottle of champagne in his hand.

'Oh, you brought your own!'

'As the Scout motto decrees, I came prepared!'

Lorraine laughed, watching as he deftly uncorked the bottle and poured two brimming glasses, then raised his in a silent toast to her.

She sipped the delicious, bubbly liquid, her liking for him increasing as he produced a bottle of grape juice for the children, and served them with a solemnity that brought a lump to her throat. How kind and sensitive he was to a child's needs! He'd make a wonderful father.

'I'se hungry,' Jilly announced.

'You always are!' Jason headed for the kitchen, drink in hand. 'But luckily for you I've been slaving over a hot stove all day!'

Giggling, the children rushed after him. As Lorraine went to help remove the dishes from the oven, he waved her away, airily informing her that she was a lady of leisure tonight.

'A very admiring one,' she commented, eyeing the crisp spare ribs, Peking duck and pancakes, rice noodles and the glistening mound of vegetables he set before them. 'You really *have* been slaving!' His eyes didn't quite meet hers, and the truth dawned. 'Where from?' she asked, *sotto voce*.

'The Bamboo House.'

She was staggered. She had been taken to its counterpart in New York and knew this meal had cost him an arm and a leg. Once again it brought home to her how successful he was. Too successful to waste

his time on an incompetent glamour girl and two
children. Yet that was what he was doing, and she
felt oddly elated.

'It was very sweet of you, Jason,' she said sin-
cerely. 'I really appreciate it.'

'That makes it worth while.'

Their eyes met and colour bloomed in her cheeks.
Hastily she served the children, then herself. Silence
reigned as the sharp edge of hunger was appeased,
but soon Jilly and Paul were chattering away to Jason,
who answered their questions as seriously as if he were
talking to adults.

'I want another spare rib,' Jilly demanded, waving
her fork in the air.

As Lorraine went to give her one, Jason's hand
stopped her. 'You've forgotten the magic word, Jilly.'

'What word?'

'Please!' Paul shouted triumphantly. 'She always
forgets to say it, but Lorri never minds.'

'Jilly won't forget from now on.' Jason smiled. 'Will
you, sweetheart?'

'No,' the little girl replied, so abashed that Lorraine
bent to caress her.

As she straightened she met Jason's eyes and saw
the grey darken—could it be with desire? Nervously
she looked away.

'May I have some more duck in a pancake?' Paul
asked.

'One duck in pancake coming up,' Lorraine joked,
and prepared it for him.

'And for me,' said Jason, holding out his plate.

'Say please,' she retorted, and the children screamed
with delight as he went down on his knees and hung
his head in shame.

Positive he had deliberately forgotten the word, she knew an insane desire to lean over and hug him. Heavens, if she didn't watch out, she'd be falling for him!

By eight-thirty the table looked as though a swarm of locusts had descended on it, and Paul and Jilly were struggling to keep their eyes open.

'Time for bed,' Lorraine stated.

'Will you tell us a story?' they cried in unison.

She smiled her assent and, taking each by the hand, headed for the stairs.

'I'll clear up and then let myself out,' said Jason.

'Please don't go—don't go washing up,' she amended hurriedly, not wanting him to think she was asking him to spend the rest of the evening with her.

'Will *you* read to me like my daddy used to?' Paul called to him.

'Of course,' he said instantly. 'I'll be up soon.'

Lorraine was in the middle of reading *The Wind in the Willows* when he came into the children's room, and Paul immediately delved under his pillow and held out a book. 'This was Daddy's favourite.'

Lorraine vacated the chair for Jason and went to stand by the window. His deep voice recounting a grisly tale of adventure in the Amazon was the only sound in the room, and when he finally came to the end of a chapter Paul and Jilly were fast asleep.

Silently she moved over to kiss them, wondering what it would be like having her own husband and children. A husband like Jason. The thought was so startling that she stumbled, and his arm shot out to support her, which only added to her emotional turmoil. Afraid he would feel her trembling, she hurriedly pulled away and went down to the kitchen, which was as sparkling clean as a show house.

'You didn't order a kitchenmaid from the restaurant as well, did you?' she jested, anxious to lighten the mood as Jason came in.

'Cleaning up was all my own work!' He bowed. 'But if you'd care to make the coffee...'

'Of course. And I promise it's better than my tea!'

She was carrying in the tray when the telephone rang and Jason, at her nod, answered it. 'From Sydney, Australia,' he mouthed, and, mystified, Lorraine took the receiver from him.

It was several moments before she replaced it, and noticing that her eyes were sparkling with tears, he raised an eyebrow.

'Bad news, Lorraine?'

'No, but it brought back memories. It was James Hartley. He'd just heard about Edward, and called to say how sorry he was.'

Jason frowned. 'Hartley? The name rings a bell.'

'I mentioned him the first time I met you. You said you'd met an actor friend of my brother's in Australia, and I assumed it was James.'

'Ah yes, I remember.'

'Seems he's landed a big part in a British television series,' she went on, 'and is coming over to England for it. I'm looking forward to meeting him again. I was seventeen the last time.' She didn't mention that there had been an extra dimension in his attitude to her, that beneath the kid sister bit he had fancied her.

'Have a truffle,' Jason broke into her thoughts, proffering a box of Switzerland's best.

'Mmm, delicious. You're spoiling me.'

'I should imagine you're used to it.'

She wasn't sure she liked the inference, and was on the verge of saying so when the phone rang again. 'Sorry about this,' she murmured, and, though the call was important, pleaded visitors and said she'd return it in the morning.

'You needn't have minded me,' said Jason. 'I like listening to one-way conversations. It exercises my curiosity!'

'I can easily satisfy it,' she laughed. 'It was the Belinda Pearce Agency. I sent them my portfolio of pictures and asked if they could find any work for me. That was Mrs Pearce calling to say there'd be no problem.'

'Except with the children,' Jason retorted. 'You can barely cope as it is, so how will you manage if you're modelling too?'

'I'll figure something out. Loads of mothers work these days.'

'I know. But considering Paul and Jilly have just lost their parents, don't you think you should be at home with them?'

'Paul's at school full-time, and if Jilly has lunch at nursery school I won't have to collect her till two.'

'Do you need the money?' Jason questioned.

'I'm not exactly loaded,' she answered drily. 'And when I take the children to the States I'll want to move to a house in the suburbs and commute—and that means a live-in housekeeper.'

'How long have you been modelling?'

'Since I was eighteen. I'd intended going to university, but had a year to spare and spent it working my way across Europe.'

'And were discovered by a photographer while waiting on tables in Paris!'

'Amsterdam, actually! A very scruffy-looking man too, who asked me to pose for him.'

'In the nude.'

She reddened. 'I don't find that remark funny!'

Surprisingly Jason reddened too. 'Forgive me. Please go on with your story.'

'Well, Hans sent in my photo to a competition being run by one of the big fashion houses, and I won first prize. The rest, as they say, is history!'

'Were your parents pleased or disappointed?'

'They died when I was eleven,' she explained. 'But my brother was keen for me to take a degree and didn't want me to become a model. The only reason I did was to be self-supporting. Edward was still a struggling actor with a wife and baby to support, and I didn't want to be a drain on him any longer.' Her voice sank to a whisper. 'He was a marvellous brother, which is one reason why I'll never let the children go. He'd have wanted them to make their home with me.'

'I can understand how you feel,' Jason said compassionately. 'But surely your sister-in-law's family have some rights as well?'

'They forfeited it by their behaviour.'

'How?'

'They're very upper crust, and disinherited Anne when she married Edward.'

Jason rubbed the side of his jaw reflectively. 'Maybe they thought he was after her money.'

'No one could think that once they'd met him! He was the most honourable person. And so damned hard-working. By the time Jilly was born he'd made quite a name for himself and was earning big money. If he hadn't been killed——' She broke off, struggling for calm. 'Strange that he and Anne died almost exactly the way my parents did. It's almost as if it were fated.'

Jason was silent, and, guiltily aware that the happy tone of the evening was being destroyed, Lorraine changed the subject. 'Enough talk of my family— what about yours?'

'Rather unexciting, I'm afraid. I'm an only child and my father died when I was eight. My mother re-married some years later and moved to Spain.'

'Did you inherit your writing talent?'

'My father wouldn't have called it a talent! He was suspicious of writers and artists.'

Humour glinting in his eyes, Jason rubbed his jaw again. His finger made a slight rasping sound on his skin, and Lorraine wondered if he shaved twice a day when he had a date. Not that he appeared to regard her in this light!

'Ever considered engaging a housekeeper while you're in England?' he asked suddenly.

'Why should I?'

'If you do decide to do modelling, it might be the best solution.'

'And the most expensive,' she replied. 'Apart from which, they're harder to find than gold dust.'

He nodded and rose. 'Time to go. You look tired.'

She went with him into the hall, disappointed he was leaving so early. Her social life at the moment was non-existent, and she enjoyed his company.

'Thanks for a wonderful dinner, Jason, and for sparing us your time.'

'My pleasure. The kids are great.' He tapped her cheek with his finger. 'So is their aunt.'

'Thank you kindly, sir.' She gave him a broad smile, managing to keep it there till she had locked the door after him. Only then did she allow her depression rein, and returning to the living-room gave way to a burst of weeping—crying for happy times gone, and a brother and sister-in-law she would never see again.

Yet she was crying for herself too. A few weeks ago she had been an independent, glamorous career girl. Now she was a frustrated aunt caring for two children and falling under the spell of a man highly unlikely to want her.

Snap out of it, she upbraided herself. If you were in New York, among your friends, you wouldn't give Jason a second thought.

Not true, a silent voice said. No matter where you met him, you'd give him a second, third and fourth thought!

Upon which admission she mounted the stairs and went to bed.

CHAPTER THREE

JASON, continuing his role of mentor, called Lorraine next morning to say he knew a woman who would be ideal to help her with the children.

'Her name's Margaret Drummond and she's been nanny-housekeeper for various friends of mine over the years. She retired a while ago to look after her mother, but is now free and anxious to resume work.'

'Why would she want to come to *me*?' Lorraine asked. 'If she's that good, she can find a far more luxurious position.'

'I've given the kids a five-star rating!'

'And me the wooden spoon, I suppose?'

He chuckled. 'She'll be phoning you herself today to fix an appointment. Let me know how it goes.'

He hung up before Lorraine could comment, and ruefully she noted that he had left her question unanswered!

Hardly had she replaced the receiver when it rang again, and hearing the calm female voice at the other end she decided Miss Drummond was as speedy as the man who had recommended her!

The woman, when she arrived for an interview that afternoon, was fiftyish and plump, with short grey hair and a smiling face that betokened humour and intelligence.

'I've had my fill of stately homes and innumerable staff,' Margaret Drummond responded when Lorraine asked her the same question she had posed to Jason.

'I'd rather be in a household where I'm treated as one of the family.'

'I can guarantee that!' Lorraine smiled. 'Though I'd better warn you, my nephew and niece aren't easy to cope with. They've been through a difficult time and——'

'Mr Fletcher mentioned it,' Miss Drummond cut in. 'But I looked after four boisterous boys in my last job, so I've no worries on that score!'

Lorraine looked down at the bundle of references she had been given, knowing that Jason's spoken recommendation meant far more. 'I understand you know Mr Fletcher,' she murmured.

'Yes indeed. Three of my charges are godchildren of his, and he takes his position seriously. He seems very fond of *your* nephew and niece.'

As if on cue, they came bounding in from the garden, demanding their tea, and Lorraine introduced them to Miss Drummond, noting with approval that the woman greeted them with a warm smile but made no effort to win them over.

'You're very welcome to join us for tea,' Lorraine said to her as she shooed the children into the kitchen to wash their hands.

'Thank you, I'd like that.'

Margaret Drummond followed her in, and to Lorraine's amazement established a gentle authority over the children within moments. Deciding she could not let such a paragon go, she offered her the job there and then. It was accepted at once, and they agreed that she would start the very next day.

'I'm available, and you obviously need me, so why wait?' the woman smiled.

Why, indeed? thought Lorraine as Miss Drummond departed, and for the first time since returning to England, she felt as if a weight had been lifted from her shoulders. And it was all thanks to Jason. She might occasionally resent his critical attitude towards her, but she couldn't deny he had turned up trumps today.

Restraining the impulse to run next door and tell him so, she dialled his number.

'You were right about Miss Drummond, Jason,' she said without preamble. 'She seems ideal and I've engaged her. She's starting tomorrow.'

'You don't let the grass grow under your feet,' he teased.

'I shouldn't think you do either!' She hesitated, then said, 'As soon as we've established a routine, I'll invite you to dinner. I owe you one.'

'Forget it,' he said casually. 'I'm glad I could help.'

It was clear from his tone that the conversation was over, and she ended it hurriedly, unwilling for him to think she was a clinging vine. He had been more than neighbourly and she had no intention of taking advantage of it.

Margaret Drummond was indeed a treasure, and by her third day had taken firm but gentle control of the children. Jason did not put in an appearance, and Lorraine couldn't help being disappointed. He had, after all, recommended Margaret, and the least he could have done was pop in and say a brief hello.

When he finally did, it was one evening a week after their telephone conversation. Although she greeted him in a friendly manner, she was careful to keep it cool.

'Sorry not to have seen you,' he apologised, 'but I was finishing a very tricky chapter.' He didn't look as if he was lying either, for tired lines fanned out from his eyes, and fatigue paled his tan. But the faintly debauched air it gave him added to his attraction, and Lorraine was highly conscious of it.

Jason was a neighbour, nothing more, she reminded herself, and it was foolish to harbour dreams about him. After all, had he wished to further their acquaintance he would have invited her out, instead of dropping in to say hello whenever the mood took him.

'Why the downcast face?' he quizzed, moving a step closer to her.

'I've got a headache,' she lied, wondering how he'd react if she said his proximity was doing strange things to her pulse. His magnetism seemed to reach out to her with invisible fingers, and it was all she could do not to rest her head on his broad shoulders.

Of course, that was it! Broad shoulders, a refuge, someone to lean on and pour out her worries to. No wonder she was attracted to him! But once she was used to the responsibilities of Paul and Jilly she'd revert to her normal, resilient self, and be able to regard Jason with dispassion. Heavens, good-looking men were two a penny in her profession! Except that he was also charming, intelligent, thoughtful and kind; to say nothing of fairly famous and well-heeled. Heck, she'd have to be an idiot not to be bowled over by him! Trouble was, he wasn't bowled over by *her*.

'I dare say you're feeling weighed down by your responsibilities,' he went on. 'But you could always share the kids if they prove too much for you.'

'Share them?' she asked blankly.

'With their grandparents.'

'You can't be serious! Not after what I told you about them.'

He shrugged. 'They're family, even so.'

'Some family! They refused to see their daughter and wouldn't acknowledge their grandchildren.' Lorraine's voice trembled with anger. 'I'm astonished you should take their side.'

'There are two sides to every story.'

Pointedly she turned on her heel and went towards the kitchen. 'Would you care to stay to supper, Jason? Margaret's made a casserole, so I can guarantee it's edible!'

'I'd like nothing better, but I'm dining out.'

Deflated, but not showing it, she opened the front door. He walked past her, then stopped on the threshold.

'Has that model agency found you any work yet?' he quizzed.

'Yes. My first assignment's next Wednesday.'

'Let me know how it goes,' he called as he walked down the path.

Like hell I will! Lorraine thought mutinously as she closed the door. If he wants to know, he'll have to do the asking himself.

She was still fuming when Sally and Denis popped in for coffee an hour later.

'I've just seen the most gorgeous hunk of manhood leaving the house next door,' Sally commented. 'Any idea who he is?'

'My neighbour. The one I told you about.'

'The writer? But you gave the impression he was a bossy fusspot, always telling you what to do!'

'He is, and he does. Don't be carried away by his looks.'

'I'd be happy for him to carry me away any day!' Sally stated, winking at Denis to show she didn't mean it. 'I haven't seen such a divine-looking man in ages. What are you going to do about it?'

'Nothing.' Lorraine made herself give a casual shrug. 'A woman with two children is hardly likely to appeal to the Jason Fletchers of this world.'

'I don't see why. From the way this one has helped you, I'd say he likes the three of you very much.'

'Maybe he does. But that's a long way from taking us on as his family.'

'Well, at least keep the friendship going,' Sally enjoined. 'You never know what may result from it.'

'Women!' Denis muttered into his coffee-cup. 'Always matchmaking!'

'Why not?' Sally asked dulcetly. 'Happy wives want their single girlfriends to be happy wives too.'

'There's no answer to that,' chuckled Denis, and raised an eyebrow at Lorraine. 'Now Sally's decided to marry you off, you don't stand a chance!'

'I certainly don't stand a chance with Jason,' Lorraine said crisply. 'So give over, you two, and let's talk of something really important. What's happening with the Stanways?'

'I'm in touch with their lawyer,' Denis said, 'but the news isn't good. Lord Stanway is still adamant that his grandchildren should remain in Britain, and will do everything in his power to prevent them leaving.'

'Then, if necessary, I'll settle here. It will mean starting my career almost from scratch, but——'

'Don't give in yet,' advised Denis. 'My partner specialises in custody cases, and I'm hoping he'll come up with a new angle we can pursue.'

'As long as I can have Paul and Jilly, I don't mind what angle,' Lorraine stated. 'They're more important to me than anything in the world.'

CHAPTER FOUR

THE lights were soothing and warm on her body as Lorraine moved her bronze-tinted face this way and that while she performed for the photographer's lens.

'Domesticity seems to have done wonders for you,' Bud Weston joked as the scene came to an end. 'You're even more beautiful than in New York.'

Lorraine's eyes crinkled. This was her first assignment in England, and it was a stroke of luck it was with Bud, who was here for a few months and had chosen her for this job.

'Or maybe you're just happy being back in your own country,' he went on. 'But whatever, you look sensational. In fact, I'd like to take some extra shots and send them to a client.'

'I can't stay after four. I have to get back to the children.'

'I thought you had someone looking after them?' He saw her hesitation. 'Come on, Lorri, it won't take long.'

'OK. But I have to go by five.'

It was closer to six before Bud was finished, and even later than that when Lorraine let herself into the Hampstead cottage and saw Jason come out of the living-room. At the sight of his broad-shouldered figure adrenalin coursed through her, and with an effort she controlled her pleasure and forced herself to walk calmly towards him.

'Thanks for coming home,' he said sarcastically. 'According to Margaret you were due back three hours ago.'

'The session went on longer than expected. Is anything wrong?'

'I've sorted it out.'

'What happened?' Lorraine asked sharply.

'Jilly was taken ill at school and was sent home. When she found you weren't here she became hysterical, and Margaret called me over to see if I could quieten her.'

'Where's Jilly now?'

'In bed.'

Lorraine raced upstairs to where Jilly lay cuddling her teddy. Her eyes were still puffy from crying, and at the sight of her aunt she burst into tears again.

'I want Mummy!' she sobbed. 'I want Mummy!'

'I know you do, darling.' Crooning gently, Lorraine cuddled her niece close. She knew Jason was watching from the door, but was too upset to be disconcerted by his disapproving presence.

'I'm going now,' he said coldly.

'You said Jilly was ill?' she murmured over the little girl's head.

'Flu,' came the retort. 'I drove her to the doctor and he advised Paracetamol and bed. Dammit, woman, if you were going to be late, you should at least have called!'

Unwilling to argue with him in front of Jilly, Lorraine gently placed her niece back on the pillows. 'I'll be with you in a minute, darling,' she whispered, and hurried after Jason, who was at the front door.

'I couldn't telephone Margaret,' she said jerkily. 'We were taking shots in Hyde Park.'

'Don't apologise to me,' he bit out. 'I'm not the one who needs you. When I found Margaret for you I never thought you'd take advantage of it by putting work before the children.'

'That's not fair!' she protested.

'It's the way I see it. I don't blame you for wanting to carry on with your life, but for heaven's sake let the children be brought up by someone who can give them the time and attention they need!'

He strode away, and fighting back the tears Lorraine returned to Jilly. The little girl was asleep, and Lorraine went to her room and stood looking out at Paul playing in the garden. At the sight of him her anguish intensified. He was a more introverted child than his sister, and she had frequently seen tears well into his eyes when he had thought himself unobserved. It had increased her determination never to give up the children, and she still felt this despite Jason's parting shot.

Turning from the window, she glimpsed her reflection in the mirror, ruefully acknowledging that her appearance might well have contributed to his outburst. The Technicolor make-up and spiky hair-do Bud had insisted on made her look more of a punk rocker than a guardian of two youngsters. If only she'd paused to remove the goo from her face and comb her hair out before rushing home!

Doing so now, she went in search of Margaret, who was preparing supper in the kitchen. It was clear from her embarrassed expression that she had overheard part of Jason's outburst.

'I'm terribly sorry, Miss Ellis. It was wrong of me to call Mr Fletcher, but Jilly was so upset I——'

'You did the right thing, Margaret. Don't worry about it.'

Relieved, the woman bustled round the kitchen. 'We've only plain roast chicken,' she apologised. 'I was going to stuff it, but when Jilly——'

'Plain roast's fine,' Lorraine assured her truthfully, but Jason's attitude had robbed her of her appetite and she could only toy with her food. Margaret did little better, and most of the chicken was put in the refrigerator.

By ten-thirty the house was in darkness, though Lorraine found sleep impossible, and was still wide awake when a distant church clock chimed midnight. The loss of her brother had never seemed more acute, making her painfully aware of how alone she was, and she stumbled from bed and went down to make herself a soothing hot drink.

The kettle had not yet boiled when the doorbell rang. Heart thumping, she padded into the hall and peered through the narrow window beside the door. It was Jason.

'What do you want?' she called coldly.

'To speak to you.'

'At this hour?'

'I know it's late, but I saw your light go on—so let me in.'

With shaky fingers she unbolted the door and opened it, but did not let him in. Let him have his say on the doorstep! However, Jason had other ideas, and pushing the door wider he stepped past her into the hall.

'I owe you an apology,' he said abruptly. 'I was completely out of order, being so rude to you.'

'Meaning you don't think me an unloving aunt who puts her career before her nephew and niece, or that you *still* think me unfit to look after them but realise it's none of your business?'

'Meaning you aren't unloving—quite the contrary—and that you're doing your best to take care of them and keep a career going.'

This was well and truly an apology, and she smiled and relaxed. 'OK, you're forgiven.'

'A cup of coffee would prove it.'

His eyes smiled into hers, then moved lower, and she was instantly aware of her flimsy silk robe. 'I'm not dressed for entertaining,' she demurred.

'I find you *very* entertaining!'

A dimple came and went in her cheek and, tightening the sash around her waist, she led the way into the living-room and switched on the lamps. They cast a friendly glow over the chintzes and rugs, and she saw Jason stare round the room as if he hadn't seen it before.

'How peaceful it is without the children!' he murmured. 'Though you look like a child yourself in that lilac get-up, with your face scrubbed pink.' He stepped closer to her. 'I like you best this way, Lorraine,' he went on huskily, touching the ruffled neck of her dressing-gown. 'I'm glad you don't go in for sophisticated nightwear.'

'Sophisticated?' she echoed.

'Black chiffon or scarlet satin!'

She giggled. 'You're years out of date, Jason. Today's sleepwear consists of men's shirts or grandma-style nighties.'

'My grandma never wore anything like this!'

Once again a supple hand touched the soft silk, and she pulled away sharply. 'I'll make the coffee.'

'Does my being close to you make you nervous?'

'Not at all,' she lied.

'Shall we kiss and make up?' he questioned, his mouth smiling, his eyes sensuous.

'There's no need. Your apology was handsome enough.' Turning on her heel, Lorraine went into the kitchen.

He followed her, leaning against the door as she took a can of coffee beans from the cupboard. 'Don't tell me you're making real coffee?'

'Why, yes. I always do.'

He clapped a hand to his forehead. 'And here I was, taking you for an "instant" girl! Shows how wrong I was.'

'Shows you shouldn't jump to conclusions about people!'

'I never do.'

'You did with me. Why?'

'I guess I judged you on your glamorous image.'

'But I looked a wreck the first time you saw me!'

'The glamour still came through,' he asserted, 'and I couldn't see you lasting as a surrogate mother. For which I apologise.'

'Never judge a book by its cover,' she quipped. 'Looking glamorous is part of my job. Inside, I'm a homebody.'

'A very beautiful body,' he murmured, reaching for her.

She side-stepped him, feeling he was making a cheap pass at her. 'If you don't want a drink, Jason, I suggest you go home.'

'Sorry.' He returned to his position by the door, taking the tray from her as she set the coffee mugs on it.

As they left the kitchen Lorraine heard a faint cry from the children's room. With a murmured apology she dashed upstairs, her panic subsiding as she saw that both children were asleep.

'Jilly must have been dreaming,' Jason whispered behind her.

'Sometimes she gets nightmares,' Lorraine murmured. 'She misses her parents dreadfully.'

Smoothing the black curls away from the damp forehead, she lightly kissed it. As she straightened, Jason gripped her shoulders, making her overpoweringly aware of his hard, muscular body looming over her.

'I need your kisses more than Jilly does,' he whispered, pulling her close and covering her lips with his own.

His touch was tender, but when she did not draw away it grew fiercer. She was melted by the warmth of his mouth and the deepening passion he made no effort to hide. His lips caressed hers, gently parting them to give his tongue entrance, darting in and out in erotic little movements that left her in little doubt as to what he wanted to do.

She was inflamed by his ardour, the magic of his touch setting her body alight. Never had she experienced anything like this, and her desire intensified as Jason's hands ranged over her, delicately skimming her full breasts, her flat stomach, then curving round her hips to rest on her firm, small buttocks. Her robe formed only the flimsiest barrier between them and, as he continued caressing her, the material parted, giving him access to her pearly skin.

With a soft groan he found her breasts, cupping them in his palms and rotating the tips of his fingers upon her nipples. Instantly they hardened, sending a shaft of such intense desire spiralling downwards that she gasped and clung to him.

'This is no place to be making love,' he whispered into her ear.

'Nor the time, either,' she whispered back.

'Why not?'

Why not, indeed? What could she say? She was overcome by the old familiar fear of being regarded simply as a sex object, of being wanted only for her physical beauty, with no thought for the real woman behind the appealing façade. Yet surely this didn't apply to Jason? He at least knew some of her faults and weaknesses, though that didn't mean he cared deeply for her as a person.

'Let me love you,' he said thickly, seeking her mouth again.

'No.' She evaded his touch. 'I—we—we barely know each other.'

Even in the dimness of the room she saw the gleam of his teeth as he smiled. 'How much better do I need to know you for us to be neighbourly?'

'Neighbourly?' She felt as though she had been doused by iced water. 'You call making love being neighbourly?' Trembling with anger, she gathered her robe around her and ran past him.

She was in the living-room when he caught up with her and swung her round to face him. 'What's got into you, Lorraine? You can't deny there's something between us.'

Mutely she met his eyes, accepting that he spoke the truth, yet loath to acknowledge the excitement he aroused in her. Aware of it, he pulled her hard against him, pressing her so close that she felt the swell of his arousal.

'Stop dissembling,' he ground out. 'You want me as much as I want you.'

'I don't!'

'You do. You're a woman with normal, healthy desires, so why fight them?'

It was the age-old cry of a man on the make, and it angered her so much that passion died and she found it easy to pull away from him.

'I may have healthy desires, Jason, but I don't think it healthy to give in to them just because the mood takes me. So, much as I fancy you, I won't go to bed with you.'

'I'll settle for the sofa!'

Lifting her effortlessly, he carried her across to it. But the instant he set her down she pushed him violently away and jumped up.

'Jason, stop it! This isn't a joke, and I'm not flattered by your behaviour. I don't know what I've done to make you think I'd—I'd ... but I'm not that sort of girl, and if you can't accept it then I suggest you stay away.'

There was a long silence, and even in the subdued light there was no mistaking the heightened colour in his face. 'I'm sorry, Lorraine. My only defence is that most girls do these days, and I took it for granted you would too. But it won't happen again, I give you my word.' He held out his hand. 'Forgiven?'

She nodded and accepted his hand, then withdrew it quickly and went with him to the hall, where he paused and lightly kissed her cheek.

'I still fancy you like mad,' he said huskily. 'I can't lie about that!'

Before she could reply he pulled the door shut behind him, and carefully she bolted it and went upstairs.

Her body still ached for him, and her mind was a tumult of conflicting emotions that kept her wakeful for hours, mulling over everything she and Jason had said to each other since they had met.

Dawn was streaking the sky with rosy fingers before she finally acknowledged that he had infiltrated her heart, and she would be the happiest girl alive if she could spend the rest of her life with him. But would Jason ever feel the same? Nothing he had said indicated it. Indeed, he had made it plain that all he felt for her was physical desire. Still, it was a basis she could work on—for, from desire, love could grow.

Hugging the thought to herself, Lorraine finally fell asleep.

CHAPTER FIVE

IT WAS a bleary-eyed Lorraine who went down for breakfast next morning, and found a brief note from Jason waiting for her.

'Something's cropped up and I have to go out of town for a few days,' he wrote in a firm, decisive script. 'Meantime, be good!'

Resisting the urge to lock the letter away, she deliberately tore it up and dropped it into the waste-paper basket. No matter what hopes she harboured about him, it was sensible to keep them firmly under control. He was not a man who would respond to being pursued, and her best bet was to play it cool. But how difficult it was when her natural inclination was to fling herself into his arms whenever she saw him!

The first few days of his absence flew by, for she was working for Bud until the Thursday, when he flew to Rome to meet a client, and the agency had no more work for her.

'Once his photographs of you appear in *Vogue*, you'll be inundated with offers,' Belinda Pearce herself sought out Lorraine to tell her. 'But for the next month things may be slow for you.'

'I don't mind that, as long as I know the work will be coming.'

'Oh, it will, my dear. You're a natural beauty and you photograph like a dream. That's why I'm going to be very particular where we book you.'

Bolstered by Mrs Pearce's remarks, Lorraine was content to remain at home; at least, she would have been were it not for Jason who, despite saying he would be away only a few days, had been absent for the best part of ten. And not even a postcard. Yet why should he bother to send one? she rebuked herself. Trying to get her into bed didn't mean he cared for her!

Friday was Margaret's day off and, though she had thoughtfully left a chicken casserole and fresh fruit salad, Lorraine decided to make the children their favourite dessert—walnut-stuffed pancakes.

'Goody, goody!' they shouted in unison as, the main course demolished, she took the pancakes from the refrigerator and put them in the microwave to warm.

'I want mine with ice-cream,' Jilly insisted.

'I like ordinary cream,' said Paul.

'You can cover them with chicken gravy if you wish,' Lorraine teased, and the children dissolved into giggles, which a man's resonant voice interrupted from outside the kitchen window.

'What's going on in there?' it demanded.

It was Jason, and Lorraine's heart leapt with joy. But, before she could answer, Jilly did.

'Lorri made us special pancakes. Come and have some.'

'A great idea.'

He came in through the back door, six feet two of sensuous masculinity, teeth whiter than ever in a skin that had acquired a deeper tan since Lorraine had last seen him. No man had the right to be so handsome, she thought despairingly, and marvelled that her cool smile gave away nothing of her erotic thoughts.

Hurriedly she busied herself with another place setting, then put the heaped plate of pancakes in the centre of the table.

'Fantastic!' Jason exclaimed, glancing at Lorraine as he bit into one. 'Did you make these with your own fair hands, as I did our Chinese dinner?'

She laughed. 'These are really and truly mine.'

'I like it when Lorri cooks for us,' Paul interposed with such pride that she flushed with embarrassment.

'I like it best when Lorri looks after us,' Jilly piped up.

'Then I'll tell you what we'll do,' stated Jason. 'You can all spend this weekend in the country with me, and your aunt can look after all of us! Would you like that?'

Without hesitation the children shouted 'Yes!' and under cover of their noise Jason spoke to Lorraine.

'Don't look so fearful, my angel—there's no ulterior motive in my invitation. But we've a family cottage in Surrey which is unoccupied most of the time, and a change of scene will do the kids good.'

It will do *me* good too, Lorraine thought, trying to quell her pleasure at the prospect of being alone with Jason for a whole weekend. Well, certainly in the evenings! And as it was the children's half-term, they need not come back till Monday.

'Say you'll come,' he urged. 'Then I'll call Mrs Rogers—who keeps the place aired and clean—and tell her to expect us.'

Lorraine hesitated, then nodded. 'OK, when do we leave?'

'As early as you like tomorrow. We might as well have as much time there as possible.'

'I agree. Is nine-thirty too early?'

'Not for me. See you in the morning, then.'

Ruffling the children's hair, he went out the way he had arrived, leaving Lorraine staring after him in exasperation. Drat the man! He'd been away much longer than he had originally said he would, and hadn't even bothered to explain why. Of course, he didn't need to, she admitted, yet recalling his behaviour towards her the last time they had met she couldn't help feeling rebuffed. The trouble with Jason was that he blew hot and cold: one moment the pursuer, intent on sexual conquest, the next a casual friend. Well, he'd better make up his mind which he wanted to be, otherwise she'd stop seeing him.

The sun shone brightly next morning as they all clambered into Jason's Porsche. With a sly grin in Lorraine's direction he handed Paul and Jilly their own individual Walkmans, after which there was no sound from the back of the car, other than the occasional whirr as one tape was changed for another.

'You certainly understand how to manage children,' she observed.

'Not only children!' Eyebrows raised, he waited for her riposte.

But she had no intention of playing into his hands, and pretended to concentrate on the passing scene. Soon, grey streets gave way to country lanes, buses and cars were superseded by fields of cattle, and the smell of petrol fumes was replaced by fresh air scented by grass and wild flowers.

Jason turned off the air-conditioning and opened all the windows, and Lorraine breathed in deeply and feasted her eyes on cornfields and bright yellow swathes of rape swaying in the gentle breeze.

'I wish such lovely yellow flowers didn't have such a horrible name,' she mused aloud, then could have bitten out her tongue as grey eyes roamed her face.

'I hope my behaviour ten days ago didn't bring that word to mind?'

'Certainly not,' she said hurriedly.

'Good. I've never lost control of myself, though something about you that night damn near made me.'

'I'm sorry.'

'Hell! I'm the one who should apologise.' One hand left the wheel, and for an instant touched her knee. 'Your innocence saved you, my lovely Lorraine, and it will go on doing so.'

'I'm glad to hear it,' she said evenly. 'I'd hate for us not to be friends.'

'Friends? Is that all you think we are?'

'Of course. Good friends.'

'A phrase which has a variety of meanings,' he put in softly, then rounded a bend in the lane and almost immediately bumped the car down a narrow rutted track to a thatched cottage set in a gentle hollow, with a small stream bubbling alongside it.

'How fabulous!' gasped Lorraine. 'Did you say it was your family's cottage?'

'Yes. But it's rarely used since my mother moved to Spain.'

'I'm surprised you didn't decide to work here when you were looking for a bolthole.'

'Good thing I didn't, he countered, 'or I wouldn't have met you.'

Lorraine's answer was drowned by the children's squeals of pleasure as they realised they had arrived, and private conversation came to an end as she and Jason brought in the luggage and carried it upstairs.

There were three bedrooms, one each for Jason and Paul, for Jilly pleaded to share with her aunt, a wish Lorraine readily agreed to, carefully avoiding Jason's eye as she did.

'We're not far from Hampton Court,' she heard him tell Paul. 'We'll go there tomorrow and see who'll find their way out of the Maze first.'

'Jilly will be last,' Paul stated with brotherly candour.

'No, I won't,' she piped in. '*You'll* be last.'

'I won't!'

'You will!'

'How about a paddle in the stream?' Jason intervened. 'Then we'll stroll into the village and have lunch at the Red Slipper.'

Quarrel forgotten, Paul and Jilly raced into the garden and were soon splashing happily in the water, while Lorraine unpacked, then went down to the tiny but well-appointed kitchen to make coffee.

The refrigerator was full of food, and she was delighted to see a casserole, meat pie and several vegetable dishes; Jason's instructions, she was sure, and gave him full marks for consideration.

Peering through the casement window, she smiled at him splashing with the children, and was in no way surprised when the three of them had to change into dry clothes before setting out for the village.

The Red Slipper was a cosy restaurant opposite the village green, and it was a good thing Jason had booked a table, for it was packed with people, mainly foreign tourists, from their accents. The food was excellent—plain English cooking and well-prepared—and Paul and Jilly behaved exemplarily, as they always did when they were out.

'What a charming-looking family!' an elderly gentleman murmured to his wife as they walked past their table on their way out, and Lorraine, half turning to smile at Jason, saw an expression in his eyes which set her pulses hammering.

True to his word, his behaviour was faultless, and though this pleased her in one way, it didn't in another! They had an early supper—country air seemed to make them hungry—then played several highly competitive games of Ludo before going to bed. As a special treat she had allowed the children to remain up late, and delighted her niece by going to bed at the same time as she did. Strictly to please Jilly, she told herself as she slipped between the covers of the large double bed; it had nothing to do with avoiding a tête-à-tête with Jason. Nothing whatever.

Next day they went to Hampton Court. It stood on a curve of the Thames beyond Richmond, in a huge, tree-filled park, its soft red brick buildings rich with turrets and chimneys, and distinctly Tudor.

They went through the Palace itself, and though Lorraine would like to have lingered in the elegant rooms Paul and Jilly were too eager to get into the Maze.

Surprisingly, there were hardly any people there, and Paul, with some bravado, set off between the high hedges. 'I'll *never* get lost,' he asserted.

'Don't be too sure, young man,' Jason called after him.

'Keep close, Paul,' Lorraine advised, as Jilly, not as brave as her brother, clung firmly to her hand.

'Stop being an old mother hen,' Jason teased as he followed her along the narrow pathway, keeping close behind her as they twisted and turned, went back on themselves a couple of times and eventually found themselves at a small square with a bench, in the centre of the Maze.

Paul was already sitting there, puffed up with importance. 'I won! I won!'

'Not quite,' Jason contradicted. 'You have to find your way out first.'

'That's easy. Let's go, Jilly. I'll race you!'

Paul darted off, his sister hard on his heels, and as Lorraine went to follow Jason halted her with his hand.

'They won't be lost, I promise you. We'll go and find them presently.'

'I'd rather go now,' she said anxiously. 'I don't want Jilly getting nervous. Paul? Jilly?' she called. 'Where are you?'

There was no answer and, pulling free of Jason, she went after them. She had hoped to use the sun as a compass, but sitting down for a while had disorientated her and she was no longer sure of her bearings, so that after five minutes she was disconcerted to find herself back in the centre of the Maze, with no sight of her nephew and niece or Jason.

She set off again, moving more slowly, but again ended up by the bench. The hedges appeared higher than she remembered, and a sudden feeling of claustrophobia—which she hadn't had since a child—unexpectedly washed over her. Sweat sheened her forehead and her breathing quickened.

'Jason?' she called.

There was no answer, and she began to shake. She went to move forward, but her feet wouldn't obey her. Be calm, she ordered herself, you aren't in the Kalahari Desert, for goodness' sake! You're at Hampton Court, with hundreds of people around. But her panic deepened and her breathing was so shallow, she had to gulp in air fast lest she fainted. Yet the faster she breathed the worse she felt, and the scene around her started revolving.

'Lorraine, what is it?'

Miraculously Jason was beside her, and with a cry of relief she fell against his chest.

'Silly girl!' he scolded, his arms enfolding her. 'And you were worried about Jilly being nervous!'

'Where is she?'

'Outside with Paul, waiting for you.'

Secure in his arms, Lorraine looked up at him and managed a slight smile. 'I felt as if the hedges were closing in on me.'

'I'm the only one allowed to do that,' he said softly, and, bending his strong, dark face, found her mouth with his own.

Unnerved by the last few moments, Lorraine couldn't dissemble, and she responded with all the ardour of her passionate nature, pressing her body close to his, aware of his instant arousal and revelling in it.

Jason was the first to draw back, his face tender as he gently stroked her hair. 'We do have our moments,' he murmured, 'but always at the wrong time and in the wrong place!'

'Luckily!' she said shakily, smoothing her dress and trying to regain control of herself.

Giving her a wry look, he caught her hand and, with an accuracy she would have resented had she not been grateful, led her out of the maze to where Jilly and Paul greeted her as though she had returned from Mount Everest.

The sun was low in the sky by the time they left Hampton Court, and soon the children were asleep in the back of the car.

'Maybe we should wake them,' Jason suggested, 'or they'll never go to sleep at home.'

Was there an ulterior motive in his statement? Lorraine wondered. But, as she went to speak, Paul suddenly did.

'My teacher says owls hoot at night, and I'm not going to bed until I've heard one.'

'Then we'll have to find you one fast,' Jason replied.

'My teacher says they don't come out till very late,' Paul added. 'Do you stay up late, Jason?'

'It depends. Sometimes I can't wait to go to bed. You see, it depends on——'

'You can be up till nine o'clock, Paul,' Lorraine interposed quickly.

'Will you come to bed the same time as me, Lorri?' asked Jilly.

'Not tonight, darling,' Lorraine replied, not wanting Jason to think she was scared of him. 'But I won't be long after you.'

Yet, with supper over and the children ready for bed, she wished she had said 'yes' to her niece, for her physical awareness of Jason was like a flame through her body, setting her on fire for him.

'I haven't heard the owl yet,' Paul stated from the foot of the stairs.

'Pop into bed and I'll go and find one with my torch,' said Jason.

'A light might scare it away.'

'I'll only use it to see where I'm going. I won't flash it up at him!'

Satisfied, Paul went to bed, and Lorraine went in to him after she had settled Jilly.

'I haven't head the bird yet,' he informed her, sitting up straight and clearly determined to ward off sleep.

'There may not be any owls around here,' she said.

'I'm sure there are. My teacher——' He broke off as a soft hooting came from the darkness outside. 'There! My teacher was right!'

The hooting came again, louder this time, and Lorraine hid a smile at the sound of a most unusual owl, conjured out of the darkness to appease the longing of a little boy.

'I'll go to sleep now,' he announced, lying back on the pillow. 'When Jason returns, don't forget to tell him I heard the owl.'

'I promise.' Thinking how easy it was, with a little imagination, to make a child happy, Lorraine went downstairs.

Jason was coming through the front door and gave her a conspiratorial wink. 'Well, did he hear the owl?'

'Loud and clear. You almost fooled *me*!'

He looked pained. 'You mean you guessed?'

'Only because you were out of tune!'

Laughing, he waved her to the sitting-room, joining her shortly afterwards with a bottle of white wine and two glasses.

What bliss! Lorraine thought as she sank into a deep armchair and sipped the chilled Chardonnay. The cottage was silent and peaceful, apart from the pleasant crackling of logs burning in the grate, this being a typically English summer evening!

Carefully, without appearing to, she watched Jason's finely chiselled profile as he poked at the logs, sending up showers of golden-red sparks. His black hair shone as the leaping light caught it, and his wide brow, straight nose and firm mouth glowed in its flame.

She ached to kneel beside him and rest against his strength, but refused to yield to her longing. She had no intention of throwing herself at any man, least of all one who virtually anticipated it. Her heart thudded furiously as he straightened and wandered over to the music centre. Soon the haunting strains of Sibelius's Second Symphony filtered through the room, while he stood casually by the bookshelf, browsing through several volumes before selecting one. Returning to the fireplace, he stretched out on the hearthrug, and her eyes were riveted to the long muscular legs outlined beneath the well-fitting dark trousers.

'Care for something to read?' he asked unexpectedly.

'Your latest thriller?' she suggested. 'I've ordered it from the library, but there's a waiting list as long as my arm.'

'There's only one thing an author likes to hear more than that.'

'Oh?'

'That you're waiting to buy it!'

She pulled a face at him. 'I bought your last two, but——'

'Hey, I'm kidding. You don't have to apologise for not wanting to waste your money!'

'I was just explaining. In normal circumstances I'm a buyer, not a borrower, but since my brother's death I've watched what I spend.'

'I thought you said he'd provided for the children?'

'He has, but inflation's so unpredictable, I need to be careful.'

Jason rose to refill their glasses. 'Will you go all haughty on me if I give you a copy of my last opus when we get back?'

'On the contrary, I'd be delighted. How's the new one going?'

'Slowly. I have to do a lot more research.'

He sipped his wine, then set down the glass and squatted by the fire. The glowing embers shot their sparks as he poked at them once more. Lorraine, desperate to be away from the magnetic pull of the man, gave an ostentatious yawn.

'I'm flaked out. I think I'll turn in.'

'The fire's too good to leave yet. Why not sit beside me? You can't feel the warmth where you are.'

'I'm fine, thanks.'

'Then why are you shivering?' He held out his hand to her. 'I won't eat you—*or* rape you.'

She resented his condescending tone, but it would have been churlish to refuse, especially as she *was* chilly, and the embers looked most inviting. She slid down on to the rug next to him and leaned back against an armchair.

What happened next was inevitable. His arm came round her and he pulled her close against his side, then lowered his head to rest his cheek upon hers.

'You know we're right for each other,' he crooned into her ear. 'Don't fight me, darling. *Show* me you want me!'

His warm breath tickled her skin, and the musky scent of him was in her nostrils, permeating her body as she breathed. She knew she should draw back, but languor made her limbs heavy, and she offered no resistance as he tilted her chin and delicately ran his

tongue over her lips before parting them and entering
the warmth they shielded.

As his tongue, warm and sweet with wine, explored
her, she clutched at his shoulders, so giddy with flaring
passion that she made no protest when he eased her
flat on the rug and lay beside her. He feathered little
kisses over her forehead, face and neck, and his hands
skilfully unbuttoned her dress, pausing almost rev-
erently as they exposed the wisp of coffee-coloured
lace that contained the throbbing fullness of her
breasts. Gently his hands encompassed them, his
fingers encircling the rosy nipples that stiffened at his
touch.

'Jason, I——'

'Hush,' he whispered. 'Let me love you. Let me
show you how it can be between us.'

'No, Jason. I've never... I've never...'

'You're a *virgin*?'

'Yes.'

His hands dropped away from her and he eased
back, the better to study her face. What he saw in it
made his own grow tender, his mouth curving in a
whimsical smile. 'I'd never have believed it.'

'But you do, don't you? I'm not lying.'

'I realise that, darling. Your eyes speak for you.'

He bent towards her, so close that his silk shirt
brushed against her breasts, arousing her to the realisation that she was half naked. She went to draw her
dress together, but he stopped her by lowering himself
down on her, the weight of his body heavy and warm
on hers.

'Don't be frightened of me, Lorraine. I won't do
anything you don't want me to do.'

Fine words, she knew, yet they put the onus on *her*, and in her mood tonight she was likely to do something she would regret tomorrow. So how to prevent it? There was only one way, and she took it, pushing him forcibly back and scrambling to her feet.

'It isn't because I don't want to,' she said. 'I do, very much. But not like this.'

'Like this?'

'As a way of passing the time; because we're both here and fancy each other.'

'Is that all you think it is?'

'Isn't it?' she countered.

'You know damn well it isn't. We've something going between us that I don't want to spoil, and if it means my having to take cold showers till you realise it for yourself, then that's what I'll do.'

He rose, pushing his shirt back into his trousers as he faced her. They stared at one another, and his breathing deepened and quickened as he twined his arms around her. Held tightly against his body, Lorraine knew he was still aroused, the swell of his manhood pressing upon the softness of her stomach and filling her with such an intense longing that she almost drew him down on the rug again.

'I'm glad you've told me how you feel,' he went on. 'I won't deny I was all set to try my luck again, but—well, as I said before, your innocence is your protection. I'll never do anything you don't want. Just remember that.'

Filled with love, she raised her face to his, and with an incoherent murmur he took her mouth, plundering the softness within, his tongue probing deep with such fierce, penetrating thrusts that it took all her will-power not to part her legs and let him repeat the motion with the hard, throbbing muscle that pulsed vibrantly against the inner softness of her thigh.

'Oh, Jason!' She clasped her hands around his neck, cradling his head and caressing the silky black hair before running her fingers down his spine. He shuddered at her touch, and with a gasp pulled her arms away from him and broke loose. His face was suffused with colour, and sweat glistened on his brow.

'You'd better go to bed while I can still let you,' he panted. 'There's a limit even to *my* control!'

The glitter in his eyes told her he was speaking the truth, and with a whispered 'Goodnight,' she fled to the safety of her room.

CHAPTER SIX

LORRAINE shivered as she climbed naked between the cold sheets, but her heart was joyously warm as she snuggled beneath the duvet and relived the scene that had just taken place.

Jason's understanding acceptance of her refusal to give herself to him showed he was not simply interested in conquest. Indeed, he had said as much, asserting that they had something going between them which he did not wish to spoil—even if he had to take cold showers until she believed him! She chuckled at the very notion. A few more evenings alone with him, and she'd be taking a few cold showers of her own!

He would be a wonderful lover, she reflected dreamily, but equally important, his questing mind and intelligence would make him just as exciting out of bed. If only it hadn't taken the tragedy of Edward and Anne's death to bring him into her life! Sadness tinged her joy, and with a sigh she sank into slumber.

The first thing she knew was an avalanche of two laughing children descending on her, and sleepily she sluiced her face, donned a wrap and went down to make breakfast.

Jason was already in the kitchen, the luscious aroma of bacon, sizzling sausages, hot buttered toast and fragrant coffee bearing witness to his industry.

'I hope you aren't one of those females who subsist on black coffee till lunchtime?' he asked.

'Luckily, no,' she responded. 'But most females who do do it to watch their weight.'

'And you don't?'

'Not yet.'

'Then pull up a chair and tuck in!'

Breakfast over, and dressed warmly—for the day was windy and cool—they all tramped down country lanes, across stone bridges and over wooden stiles, until hunger drove them home again.

In the afternoon Paul and Jilly played in the garden while Lorraine and Jason read the papers, then argued amicably over an article on interior design.

'Personally I'd rather make my own mistakes than let a decorator loose in my home,' she declared.

'You must be very confident of your style,' he teased.

'I'm not. but I know what I like, and anyway, it's fun choosing things to buy.'

'It's the biggest bore in the world!'

She laughed, and he reached out for her hand and caressed it.

'Tell me, lovely lady, how is your apartment furnished?'

'Ultra-modern and labour-saving. Though it isn't really my style,' she added. 'I furnished it as inexpensively as possible, and promised myself I'd change things once I could afford it. Trouble was, by the time I could, I was too busy to spare the time.'

'You should have called in an interior decorator!'

She laughed, then glanced around the cosy room. 'Anyway, my apartment's too square and modern-looking for my taste, so I decided to wait until I bought myself a town house. Now, of course, it will have to be a place outside New York, but I'm rather looking forward to it.'

There was silence for several moments, and she deliberately didn't look his way.

'How will you furnish it?' he asked finally.

'It depends. But I fancy a peach bedroom, with a brass bedstead and a yellow and gold patchwork quilt.'

'You're having me on!'

'I'm not. I also want old-fashioned carriage lamps on either side of the bed!'

'And a chaise-longue at the foot of it?' he mocked, wide mouth curling upwards.

'Definitely not! I can't bear them.'

Their discussion ended on laughter, and all too soon it was five o'clock and time to leave. The journey to London was a silent one, with a tired Paul and Jilly curled up on the back seat.

Glancing back at them, Lorraine caught Jason's eye and they exchanged glances—a companionable bond between them that had no need for words. We're like a family, she thought, and experienced such pleasure that she almost blurted it out to Jason, only held back by the fear that he might think she was rushing him.

Arriving at Hampstead, he helped them in with their things, then announced that he was going out of town again for two or three days.

'To research?' Lorraine asked before she could stop herself.

'Yes.' He looked down at her, hesitated momentarily, then kissed her gently on the mouth and left.

She tried not to dwell on the disappointment of his going, hoping the time would pass quickly, but when a week had elapsed with no word from him, she began to be edgy.

'At least he could have called me,' she muttered to her reflection as she made up her face for a photographic session she had unexpectedly been asked to do, and wondered, as she had done many times before, whether she was reading too much into Jason's behaviour towards her.

The only phone call she did have was from a publicity man of the company whose clothes she had modelled for her session with Bud, inviting her out. She didn't accept, pleading another engagement, then spent the next two days fuming over Jason.

On Tuesday it was Margaret's day off and Lorraine spent the day at home. She collected the children from school and prepared their supper, and by the time they were settled for the night she was too tired and depressed to eat her own dinner. What a disaster of a summer it had been, she mused gloomily, watching the rain blur the windowpanes.

A flash of headlights caught her eye through the clouded glass, and, recognising Jason's Porsche, she jumped up and darted to the front door. But no—she wasn't going to welcome him with open arms when he hadn't even bothered to telephone her while he was away.

Tensely she waited, but it was nearly an hour before he called in to see her, drawing her into his arms and kissing her so soundly that her sour mood melted instantly, and they stood together without speaking, content to be close.

After a moment she looked up at him, taken aback to see him frowning. 'What is it?' she asked. 'Did you have trouble with your research?'

'Not really. Things will work out OK.' He rubbed his cheek upon hers. 'Miss me?'

'No.'

'I missed *you*.' He found her mouth again, and this time his kiss was hungry with passion, only gentling when he felt her response. 'You did miss me,' he said with soft triumph.

'Well . . . a little bit.'

'Good.' He released her and moved across to the sideboard. 'Mind if I pour myself a drink?'

'Go right ahead. I hope you notice I have a decent supply of sherry and a bottle of whisky?'

'I give you full marks! Shall I fix you something?'

'Not for the moment, thanks.'

Pouring himself a Scotch, Jason settled in an armchair and raked back his hair. It had grown longer and needed cutting, though she rather liked it this length. The light from a standard lamp fell full upon him and she noticed the lines of strain on his face.

'You look exhausted, Jason. I never knew research was so hard.'

'It isn't usually.'

'Care to talk about it?'

'I'd rather not. Tell me what *you've* been doing with yourself.'

'I had one day's work and spent the rest of the time with the children.'

'You shouldn't build your life around them,' he said.

His remark startled her. 'But they're a part of my life; they always will be.'

'I understand that. But they need two people to look after them.'

Colour bloomed in her face, but she managed to speak in an expressionless voice. 'If you mean they need a father, then you're right. But for the moment we're a one-parent family and there's nothing I can do about it.'

She waited tensely for his comment, convinced he had turned the conversation this way to ask her to marry him. Joy coursed through her, strong as the headiest wine, so that his next sentence—when it came—was a total let-down.

'What about their grandparents? I still think it reasonable that they should have a hand in their upbringing.'

His words shattered her dreams and she reacted violently. 'How can you even suggest such a thing? You're aware of the situation: the way they ignored their daughter, wouldn't even acknowledge Paul and Jilly!'

'But you told me they'd had a change of heart, and in that case, it would relieve you of a hell of a lot of responsibility.'

'I don't need to be relieved of it.' With a struggle Lorraine curbed her anger. 'To be honest, I'm hoping they've abandoned the idea of trying to gain custody of them. I've been meaning to call Denis to see if he has any news.'

'I'm sure they're still wards of court,' Jason observed, 'so you can't take them to the States.'

'If necessary I'll——' She broke off and glanced through the window as a car shrieked to a stop outside. 'Know anyone with a white Lotus?' she asked Jason.

'What?' Coming to stand behind her, he peered over her shoulder, then with a muttered 'Excuse me, will you?' dashed from the house and strode down the path.

As he did, a slim, dark-haired young woman stepped from the car, flung her arms around his neck and kissed him on the mouth.

Lorraine stepped back from the window as if it were on fire. Fool! she berated herself. Did you think you were the only girl in his life? That he's never made love to another woman, never said he desired them, wanted to go to bed with them? Sick at heart, she retreated to the kitchen and poured herself a coffee, walking agitatedly around the room as she tried not to think of Jason.

She was still seething when some half an hour later he returned with the girl in tow. Close up, she was older than Lorraine had thought, being in her late twenties. But she was also prettier, with a tiny, curvaceous body, English rose skin and large brown eyes. And as if that weren't enough, her hair was glossy black and curled tantalisingly around her well-shaped head.

'I'd like you to meet Erica Robson,' said Jason. 'My publisher's right-hand whip! She's here to check how my book's progressing.'

It seemed a somewhat untimely hour to do this, and Lorraine doubted that Jason was being wholly truthful. But she knew better than to say so, or even hint it, and gave Erica a welcoming smile as she led the way into the living-room and offered them a drink.

'I'll see to it,' Jason said easily, and strolled over to the drinks tray, leaving Lorraine no option but to sit down opposite the girl.

Her job must be highly paid, she thought. Either that, or she had private means—or a rich boyfriend. Lorraine refused to dwell on the latter. Whatever, the cream silk Armani suit with its exquisitely embroi-

dered collar and cuffs would have given no change
from five hundred pounds.

'Jason was telling me why you had to return to
England.' Erica spoke for the first time, her voice clear
as crystal, but hard as a diamond.

Not a pretty voice, Lorraine was bitchily pleased to
hear, and she said softly, 'It was an awful shock for
me, but I'm just beginning to come to terms with it.'

'You're very brave, coping with two youngsters.
What about your sister-in-law's family, can't they help
out?'

'No,' Lorraine said flatly, unwilling to air private
grievances. Glancing up to accept the sherry Jason
was proffering, she noticed the quick glance he flung
Erica, and was convinced he had already disclosed
the reason to the girl. It made her all the more positive that she was more than the 'publisher's whip' in
his life.

'They're great kids,' he interposed, sinking down
on to the sofa. 'There's never a dull moment with
them.'

'How domestic you sound, darling,' Erica teased.
'I'm delighted to hear it!'

'Have you two know each other long?' Lorraine
asked lightly, deciding there had been enough talk
about children and she might as well glean what information she could.

'Years and years,' Erica replied.

'Only since I've been writing,' Jason said
simultaneously.

'Well, that's years and years,' Erica put in.

Lorraine sensed an undercurrent of tension between the two of them, and her curiosity deepened,
as did her disquiet. It made her realise how little she

knew about the man she had fallen in love with, other than what she had read on the jacket of his latest novel. True, he had mentioned that his mother and stepfather lived in Spain, but had said nothing of his personal life or how he saw his future. Was he a perennial bachelor, who loved and left, or had he had any long-standing relationships? More important, how did *she* figure in his life? There were moments when she believed she knew, but many more when she knew she didn't!

'I'm starving,' Erica said into the silence. 'I thought you were taking me to dinner, Jason.'

'Ready when you are.' He jumped to his feet and glanced at Lorraine. 'Care to join us?'

It was not the most enthusiastic invitation she had ever received, and she was glad she had a genuine excuse for turning it down.

'I'm afraid I can't. It's Margaret's day off.'

'Ah, yes, so it is.'

'It was lovely meeting you,' Erica said from the door. 'I'm sure we'll meet again.'

Not if I can help it, Lorraine thought as she watched them drive off. There was something about the girl that made her hackles rise. And not only because she seemed too close to Jason!

Dejectedly she went into the kitchen for another cup of coffee. She hadn't eaten anything since lunch, but was nauseated by the idea of food. All she could think of was Jason: what he had grown to mean to her, and how empty her life would be without him.

CHAPTER SEVEN

NEVER had a night been so long. Lorraine courted sleep as avidly as a lovesick swain his lady, but one o'clock came and went and she was wide awake as a cricket.

At one-thirty she heard the sound of Jason's car—Erica's Lotus having been left outside his house when they had gone out to dinner—and she waited to hear it spark into life as the girl drove away. What she heard instead were two sets of footsteps up the path and the slam of the front door.

Jealousy twisted her gut, and pushing aside the duvet she padded over to the window-seat, careful to keep herself hidden by the curtain. A dim light came from Jason's living-room; too dim, she thought bitterly, and had a painfully vivid picture of Erica's pliant body curving into his muscular one.

How long had they been lovers? It was patently obvious, from the way Erica had looked at him, that they were. Or at least *had* been. But that didn't mean their affair was still going on. She couldn't believe Jason would play fast and loose with two women at the same time.

Hugging this thought to herself, she remained by the window, steadily growing colder and colder. Her limbs were all but numb when steps sounded on the path, and peering round the curtain she saw Jason help Erica into her car.

Lorraine was in the middle of breakfast next morning when he telephoned. It was so unusual for him to do this—when he wanted to talk to her he always popped in—that her heart raced like a piston, convinced he was going to say something about Erica that would destroy all her hopes.

On the contrary. What he said raised them sky-high, for he invited her to have dinner with him that evening, and ordered her to put on her best bib and tucker because they were celebrating.

'Celebrating what?' she asked.

'Having known each other seven weeks!'

Promising to look her most glamorous, Lorraine returned to the kitchen, Erica firmly relegated to the past.

Anxious as a schoolgirl on her first date, she changed her dress three times before she was satisfied with her choice—red chiffon, and figure-fitting as a surgeon's glove. It turned her into a *femme fatale*, and to heighten the image she sculpted her hair away from her face into a smooth golden crown, pinning it in place with tiny, diamond-studded grips. The total result was dramatic enough to need no further enhancement, and she applied her make-up with a light hand, aware that excitement gave her skin and eyes lustre.

Promptly at eight, Jason arrived. Adonis, she thought, staring into his handsome face, conscious all the while of his lean, hard body.

'You're beautiful,' he breathed, drawing her into his arms and inhaling the scent of her. 'I've missed you like hell.'

'You only saw me yesterday.'

'For a few minutes.'

'It wasn't my fault you went off with Erica,' she said lightly, determined not to let him know the anguish he had caused her.

'Erica isn't a lady one can lightly dismiss. And she did have good reason to wave the whip. I promised Jim—my publisher—he'd have my book a month ago, and it's still not finished.'

'Didn't you explain that you're still researching it?'

'Yes, but he knows that unless Erica bullies me, I'll keep rewriting.'

'I can't imagine you allowing any woman to bully you.'

'Not any woman,' he agreed, leading her out to the car. 'But I'm an absolute sucker where *you're* concerned.'

Lorraine refused to take him seriously, though she wished she could, and was on the verge of saying as much, when she decided against it. Let Jason make the first move and she'd come clean about her feelings for him. Until he did, she'd say nothing.

The restaurant he took her to was too new to be in any of the guide-books, but too pretty to be out of it for long.

'A few more months and you'll have to book weeks in advance,' Jason grunted as they settled themselves at a table on a flower-filled terrace, with the main restaurant behind them.

'Nothing good can be kept secret for long,' she agreed.

'I wouldn't say that.'

An undercurrent in his voice alerted her, and she looked at him closely.

'I've kept my feelings for *you* secret,' he went on, leaning across the table. 'Though anyone seeing me with you tonight would guess how I feel.'

'*I* can't,' said Lorraine, not sure how seriously to take him. Jason was adept with words—it was his profession, after all—and it was all too easy to read more into them than he meant.

'Don't you really understand what I'm trying to say?' he asked.

'I think so, but I'm not sure if you'd say the same tomorrow or the day after!'

'I'm looking to the future, if that's what you mean. I——'

He broke off as a waiter approached to take their order, and they both chose their meal so hurriedly that Jason chuckled as the man moved off.

'We should have gone for McDonald's, for all the attention we'll be giving to the food tonight!'

Lorraine grinned back and pretended to rise, and he caught her hand, the humour leaving his face as he felt the soft texture of her flesh.

'Do you think I'm only interested in a one-night stand, Lorraine?'

She shrugged. 'That seems to be the norm these days.'

'Not for me.' His tone was clipped. 'Not for any thinking person. And it's certainly not my intention with *you*. I love you, Lorraine. I did from the first day we met.'

'In my dirty apron and with my food-spattered face?'

'Absolutely.'

'Why didn't you tell me before?'

'Because I couldn't believe it. It had never happened to me before. I've had affairs, but always knew they'd never be more than that. But with you—when I saw you on the doorstep with the children—it was as if I was seeing my future.'

Lorraine had waited so long for Jason to say this that she couldn't take it in.

Misinterpreting her silence, he said sharply, 'What about you? You respond when I kiss you, but——'

'I've loved you for ages,' she burst out, 'but I was scared to show it in case you thought I was running after you.'

'You wouldn't have had to run far,' he said thickly, and glanced round the room. 'Damn! We should have had this conversation before we came here. I can't wait to get out and hold you!'

Knowing he meant it she delighted in the power it gave her. Who would have thought Jason, always in control of himself, would behave this way?

'I'm a quick eater,' she said softly.

'Me too.'

They looked at each other and laughed.

'I don't think anyone's ever been in and out of this restaurant as fast as us,' he commented an hour later as they stood on the steps, waiting for the doorman to bring round their car.

'We'll have to go back there,' she said. 'I'm sure the head waiter thought us crazy, leaving half the food untouched.'

'The wine waiter didn't,' Jason informed her. 'From the way he tried to look down the front of your dress, he must have guessed exactly what I had in mind!'

Lorraine glanced down at herself. The bodice was low-cut, but not outrageously so. 'Is it really too low, Jason?'

'No, my darling. But with such a fabulous figure, even in a sack you'd arouse a corpse—and the waiter was alive and Italian!'

She giggled, enjoying Jason in his teasing mood, and facing up to the fact that when they were alone she would have to reach a decision. Yet she knew what the decision would be, and that all the times she had said no had been because of this one moment, because of this one man who had entered her world when it had been turned upside-down, and who, by his kindness, understanding and sheer bossiness, had righted it.

'Why so quiet?' he asked as they drove towards Hampstead.

'I was thinking about us.'

'Am I permitted to ask what the thoughts were?'

'Just how lucky it is we met.' She longed to talk of their future, but caution restrained her. Though Jason had said he loved her, he hadn't asked her to be his wife, and might only be thinking in terms of a live-in relationship.

She bit back a sigh, recognising that she was caught in a quandary that had troubled her since men had first started regarding her with desire: how to equate her own personal moral standards with those of a world that was very different. Would she be happy living with Jason without the commitment of marriage? Somehow she didn't think so, for if he was unwilling to make those vows...

She became aware of the car slowing down and, giving him a sidelong glance, found him watching her with a quizzical expression.

'Worried I'll let you down, Lorraine?'

His insight took her aback, but made it easier for her to reply. 'Not exactly let me down, but—but we don't really know each other all that well.'

'I know you very well.' He turned into the cul-de-sac where they lived and drew the car to a stop between their two houses. 'Have you ever been let down by a man?' he asked unexpectedly.

'No. I've never given one the chance. They've always been too obvious in what they wanted from me.'

'Yet you let *me* get close, and I think I've been equally obvious.'

She turned in her seat, scanning his finely boned face and wishing it were possible to scan his mind. 'My feelings for you sort of crept up on me,' she confessed.

'I won't hurt you, darling.' His voice was rough with passion, and he slid across the seat and put his arms around her, muttering as the gear lever dug into his thigh. 'I do choose my moments, don't I?' he said ruefully. 'I haven't made love to a girl in a car since my undergraduate days!'

She couldn't help smiling, understanding his frustration because she was experiencing it too. 'I've a perfectly good sitting-room going vacant,' she informed him.

'With Margaret and the kids ten feet above our heads?' he quizzed. 'No. I prefer *my* sitting-room.' Her hesitation was too noticeable for him to ignore. 'What I said to you back in the cottage still holds, my sweet. I'd never force you to do anything you didn't want.'

The trouble was, she did want—desperately, and she knew that if she was alone with him in his home and they started making love she wouldn't want him to stop. Was that so wrong? she wondered. After all, they loved one another, and he *had* said that from the moment he had first seen her he had seen his future. Surely that was commitment enough?

Suddenly weary of the emotions warring within her, she decided to let things take their natural course. She loved Jason and he loved her, and if there was no trust between them they had nothing.

Gently she eased away from him and opened the car door. 'Let's make it *your* house,' she whispered, and heard his quick, indrawn breath.

They were walking together up his path when they heard a child's cry, high and piercing, from next door, and seconds later saw the light in Jilly's bedroom flash on.

'Mummy, Mummy!' came the wail, and Lorraine stopped in her tracks.

'Oh, heavens, she's having another nightmare!'

Jilly's cry came again, and Lorraine looked at Jason wordlessly.

'OK,' he said ruefully.

Gratefully she touched her fingers to his cheek before running across to her own house. As she let herself in and raced upstairs, Jason was directly behind her, though he waited at the bedroom door when he saw Margaret kneeling by Jilly's bed and cuddling her.

At the sight of Lorraine, the little girl flung herself into her arms and burst into another storm of weeping that took several moments to quell. But eventually she was back in bed, with Lorraine and Jason sitting either side of her.

'Do you think you can go to sleep?' Lorraine asked softly.

'May I go into *your* bed?'

'But, darling——'

'*Please*, Lorri!' The dark eyes, so like Anne's, melted Lorraine's heart, and she gathered her niece close.

'Of course you may, darling,' she said huskily, and, as she went to lift her, Jason scooped the small figure from her arms and carried the child into the room opposite, where he carefully placed her on the bed. Straightening, he raised an eyebrow at Lorraine.

'Three in bed is definitely not my scene,' he muttered under his breath.

'I'm sorry, Jason. I——'

'Forget it,' he said swiftly. 'We've all the tomorrows, my darling.' Gently he kissed her lips. 'Don't bother seeing me out.'

The door closed behind him, and, trying not to think of what might have been, Lorraine—who had shared a bed with Jilly in the cottage and knew what was ahead!—prepared herself for a restless night.

CHAPTER EIGHT

AFTER spending most of the night with her niece either throwing an arm across her or kicking her in the stomach, Lorraine was still fast asleep when Margaret came in at eight-thirty to say she was wanted on the telephone.

'How's Jilly?' asked Lorraine, groggily sitting up.

'Bright as a button, and having breakfast in the kitchen.' Margaret plugged the telephone into the wall socket and held out the receiver.

It was the Belinda Pearce Agency. Mrs Pearce herself, so Lorraine knew it was important.

'I've marvellous news for you, my dear. Linda Joyce——' the woman named a top model '—has broken her leg, and Rowena, who were about to sign her up on a two-year contract, are desperately looking for a replacement. I've suggested *you*.'

Lorraine was instantly wide awake. Rowena was a leading fashion house and spent a fortune in advertising. To be their model would launch her into the big time and stand her in good stead wherever she lived.

'When do they want to see me?' she asked.

'They'll use you for a modelling session today, and if they like you, you'll be in! So put on your skates, and be at the Metropole Hotel in Brighton by eleven.'

Lorraine glanced at her watch and leapt from bed. 'Anything else I should know?'

'Only that you'll be there overnight. They want to do some night shots with the sea as a backdrop.'

'Can I return to London directly afterwards? Brighton's so near and it seems——'

'The booking includes the whole of tonight. What's the problem, my dear?'

'I don't like leaving my nephew and niece.'

'I thought you had an excellent woman taking care of them?'

'I have, but——'

'Then let her get on with her job while you carry on with yours!'

Knowing Mrs Pearce's comments were justified, Lorraine gave in.

'You'd better pack something glamorous,' the woman added. 'Larry Pethco, Rowena's publicity director, will probably take you all out to dinner.'

To Lorraine's relief, Jilly made no demur when told her aunt would be away overnight, and, as Paul had already left for school, she made a mental note to call him in the evening.

That only left Jason. He would be disappointed at not seeing her tonight and taking up where they had left off. Still, it was only a postponement, and would make their coming together all the sweeter.

'Mr Fletcher left a note for you,' said Margaret, coming into the room as Lorraine was packing. 'He slid it under the door and it must have slipped inside the morning paper. I found it only this minute.'

Her first love letter from Jason! With shaky fingers Lorraine opened the envelope and unfolded the single sheet of paper, disappointment engulfing her as she saw only two brief lines.

'Fate is conspiring against us! Urgent family business. Back in two days. Love, Jason.'

Not an affectionate letter despite the 'Love, Jason'. Sombrely she put it in her holdall, locked her case and went down to wait for the taxi Margaret had ordered.

Lorraine had never been to Brighton, and found it to be a Regency version of Atlantic City. Certainly the sea had the same cool, windy look to it.

The Metropole was one of the largest hotels, its red-brick façade facing the wide promenade. As she crossed the high-ceilinged foyer where marble ran riot, a thickset man in his late thirties, with slick black hair and darting brown eyes, intercepted her.

'Miss Ellis?' At her nod he held out a hand. A heavy gold ring adorned his finger and a bracelet watch his wrist, while a gold pendant glinted in the mat of hair his half-undone shirt disclosed. 'I'm Larry Pethco. I'm——'

'Publicity director of Rowena,' she intercepted, instantly recognising his type and knowing he'd be pleased to think she knew who he was.

'I see you've heard of me.' His smile was wider.

'Everyone in the fashion business has,' she lied.

Swelling with self-importance, he accompanied her to Reception. 'The other models are already on the beach,' he said, 'so go over there as soon as you can.' His eyes raked her. 'Belinda Pearce wasn't exaggerating when she said you were lovelier than Linda. Your colouring's the same, but you're far sexier.'

Sensing she was going to have trouble with this man, Lorraine felt her heart sink. She only hoped the evening session would go on too long for him to include taking them all out to dinner.

Excusing herself, she went to her room. It was large and airy and had a sea view. Opening the window, she leaned out. No golden sands here, but grey stones and a fresh breeze to whip the sea and bring the tangy smell of ozone to her nostrils. She breathed deep. There was something about the ocean that soothed and vitalised her at one and the same time, and she wished Jason was with her.

Ruminating on the disappointing end to last night, she picked up her make-up box and went in search of the other models.

By noon, shooting was well under way. A large van served as their changing-room, and there was a highly organised woman in charge of the clothes and accessories, and a make-up artist and hairdresser to ensure that their looks matched the various outfits they modelled.

Peter Rolls, the director, was a quiet-spoken young man who shot every picture the way Larry Pethco wanted, then re-shot them his own way every time the man was called to the telephone.

'You're lucky Larry's in such demand,' Milly Smith, one of the models, cracked when he went off for the fourth time.

'His secretary's my sister-in-law,' Peter said blandly, 'and she calls him whenever something crops up that she can't deal with.'

Nobody commented, though the smiles that passed between everyone spoke volumes.

With an hour's break for lunch, the shooting continued till the sunlight faded, when Peter called a halt, said dinner was in the main dining-room at seven-thirty, and would they all be ready to resume shooting at nine.

'I've booked us a table at the Barlow Inn,' Larry Pethco protested. 'Delay the shoot a couple of hours.'

'And run the risk of the wind coming up?' Peter parried. 'It's been forecast for late this evening.'

Disgruntled, Larry gave in, and Lorraine, conscious of him eyeing her, hurried to her room.

She was emerging from the shower when the telephone rang, and was on the verge of answering it when she stopped herself. Other than Margaret and the agency, no one knew she was here, so it had to be Larry.

As the ringing ceased, she dialled home to speak to Paul, breathing a sigh of relief to hear all was well. But no sooner had she replaced the receiver when it rang again, and she glowered at it. Concluding that Larry might call round to see her, she dressed in record time and, still buckling the belt of her cream shirtwaister, joined the crew in the bar. No sooner was she seated than Larry came in and made a beeline for her. The impeccable cut of his tan suit did little to improve his appearance: his hair was still too greasy and slick, his jewellery too obvious, his smile too lecherous.

During dinner he commandeered Lorraine's attention, and she was relieved when it was time to resume shooting.

It was cool and fresh on the beach, and she and the other two models sat in the changing van while the scene was set and lighting adjusted. Larry had disappeared, and without him work went faster, so it was shortly after ten when Peter called, 'Wrap it,' and they were free to go.

Keeping close to the other two girls, Lorraine re-turned to the hotel, her heart sinking as Larry bounded towards them in the foyer.

'We're all going to the night-club,' he announced, 'so hurry up and change.'

'I'm too tired to go out,' said Lorraine, deliberately slouching.

'Who said anything about going out?' Larry knuckled her under the chin. 'The night-club's in the hotel.'

'I don't——'

'We'll meet you there in half an hour,' Milly's en-thusiastic voice drowned Lorraine's as she pulled her towards the lift. 'What's with you?' she hissed as the doors closed behind them. 'Trying to ruin your hope of becoming the "Rowena Girl"? Put Larry's nose out of joint and you'll never work for the company again!'

'I'd rather *that* than suck up to him!'

'You're a big girl, honey; you can take care of yourself.'

But Lorraine wasn't so sure when she found herself pressed against Larry's body on the crowded night-club floor. If only she hadn't heeded Mrs Pearce's advice about bringing along her most glamorous dress! It was difficult playing down the curves of her body when supple black taffeta clung to every indentation, and with the back cut away to the waist she didn't even have the comfort of a bra to protect her from his X-ray eyes and roving hands.

Ah, well, another few dances and she'd leave, re-gardless. No job was worth pandering to the Larry Pethcos of this world. She tried to ease away from him, but the movement only served to make him tighten his hold on her, and one hot, damp palm moved slowly up and down her spine.

'I like your hair long and loose like this,' he said thickly. 'Is the colour natural?'

'Yes.'

He nuzzled his face into the soft waves, giving her a whiff of alcohol-laden breath. 'How about you and me slipping away somewhere together? I've a bottle of champagne in my room.'

Heat flooded her body. Damn him! Enough was enough. 'It's late, Larry, and I'm leaving for London early in the morning.'

'Just a quick drink,' he persisted.

'I'd rather not.' She paused, then plunged on, 'I don't want to give you false ideas, and—and if you're looking for a playmate...'

'You don't play?' he finished.

'No.'

'I'm glad to hear it.'

'You are?' She didn't believe him.

'Sure. I don't want a girl who sleeps around. You're a lady—knew it the minute I saw you. That's why I fell for you. You're beautiful and classy and intelligent enough to know I can help you. With me behind you, you can go a long way.'

All the way back to London, she decided there and then. If there was a train running tonight, she'd pack and leave.

'I could go overboard for you, honey,' Larry whispered in her ear, his soft tongue licking it wetly.

She shivered with revulsion and, misreading it, his breathing quickened and he pulled her closer against his body. She wanted to claw at him, to rake her nails down his face and draw blood, but, controlling herself, she closed her eyes tightly and counted to ten.

Jason, she thought longingly, if only you were here with me! She opened her eyes again and astonishingly found herself staring directly at him! But he wasn't alone. Erica was draped all over him.

Lorraine clamped her lids shut. She was hallucinating. She had to be! Jason couldn't be here, and definitely not with Erica.

But he was. Lifting her lids, she saw it had been no wild imagining, but inescapable fact. And Erica *was* in his arms!

His letter this morning had said he'd been called away on family business, so how come he was dancing cheek to cheek with his publisher's assistant? Or would he say she was his long-lost cousin?

Yet as misery engulfed her, logic took over. As she was judging Jason, so he could be judging her and wondering what she was doing in a night-club with an oily character like Larry! Which went to show the danger of jumping to conclusions.

Unfortunately, Jason's furious expression indicated his verdict—and no need to guess what it was!

Lorraine found the rest of the evening purgatory. Larry was as obnoxious at the table as on the floor, rubbing his knee against hers and trying to slide his hand along her thigh. Only Milly's warning glance stopped her pouring her coffee over his head, though her restraint had nothing to do with winning the Rowena contract, for she would never accept it if it meant working with this octopus.

'Another dance?' he asked, swaying to his feet.

'I'll powder my nose first.' She was up and away before he had a chance to reply.

Only as she moved towards the exit did she realise she had to pass the table where Jason was sitting with Erica and another couple. Luckily she was too well-trained for her steps to falter, and she glided forward, suspending her feelings as she sometimes did on the catwalk in a dress show.

'Good evening,' he drawled, half rising as she came abreast of him. 'I didn't know you were working in Brighton.'

'I didn't know myself till my agency rang me this morning. How is it *you're* here?'

'I'm staying nearby with some relatives.'

'Is Erica one of them?' Lorraine regretted the question the instant it slipped out, though Jason appeared amused by it, one eyebrow rising mockingly as his gaze wandered to the table she had just left.

'Friends of yours?' he drawled.

'Hardly. The man I was dancing with is publicity director of the fashion house I've been modelling for.'

Hiding her anger under a bright smile, she sauntered off, though once in the cloakroom she collapsed trembling on a chair in front of the mirror.

It was there that Erica found her, coming into the room with a rustle of silk skirt. The girl was very pretty, Lorraine conceded with a jaundiced eye. It was unusual to have creamy pink skin with such black hair, and the riotous way it curled around her head gave her a gamine look that did not match the hard brown eyes.

'What a surprise, seeing you,' Erica said, peering into the mirror as she added another coat of crimson to her pouting mouth.

'I'm on a job.'

'Me too. Jason's weeks late with his new manuscript, and I have to ensure he finishes it by hook or by crook.'

'It must help being part of his family.'

'His family?' Erica seemed startled, though she recovered fast. 'I'm not really. But we were neighbours years ago, and have been close ever since.' She smoothed her dress. 'When are you returning to the States?'

'I'm not sure,' Lorraine said casually. 'I enjoy living here.'

'Especially with Jason next door!' Erica added. 'He's very fond of the children.'

'They're equally fond of him.' Lorraine rose and walked out, convinced Erica had followed her in here simply to pry into her relationship with Jason.

Returning to the smoky atmosphere of the nightclub, she took a moment to adjust to the dimness. As they did, she saw Jason dancing with the other girl in his party, which at least spared her the necessity of walking past him.

Larry came towards her before she reached their table, swinging his hips and nodding towards the floor.

'No more dancing for me,' she said apologetically. 'I'm exhausted.'

'No problem, honey. I'm tired myself. I'll go with you.'

Anxiously Lorraine looked round for Milly, but she was engrossed talking to Peter; deeming it wiser not to make a fuss, she allowed Larry to escort her from the night-club.

'Have to see the little lady to her room,' he joked, coming into the lift with her.

'There's no need,' she said easily. 'You said you were tired.'

'Not too tired to be a gentleman.' They emerged on the second floor and he walked with her to her room, taking the key from her hand before she could stop him.

He had difficulty inserting it and she restrained a desire to snatch it back. Larry was drunk, and, though he was amiable with it, drunks had a habit of becoming tetchy.

At the third attempt he managed to open the door, and she grabbed the key from him and sped into the room. But not fast enough, for he weaved in after her.

'Mind if I sit down?' he asked thickly. 'I don't feel so good.'

He wasn't lying either, she saw, for he had lost his ruddy colour and was a sickly shade of yellow. Bending his head to put the key in the lock obviously hadn't agreed with him.

'You're better off going to your room,' she said.

'I'll never make it.' Holding his hand to his mouth, he looked wildly around.

Hastily Lorraine pointed to the bathroom, and he staggered into it and slammed the door behind him.

Furious with him, and equally furious with herself for having been inveigled into this stupid situation, she walked nervously around the room until he finally emerged—pale and contrite—and slumped into the nearest chair.

'This has never happened to me before,' he mumbled.

'Not to worry,' she forced herself to say, though it was impossible to feel any sympathy for him.

DOUBLE YOUR ACTION PLAY...

"ROLL A DOUBLE!"

Peel off label & place inside

CLAIM UP TO 4 BOOKS
PLUS A 20k GOLD-PLATED CHAIN
PLUS A MYSTERY BONUS GIFT

ABSOLUTELY FREE!

SEE INSIDE..

NO RISK, NO OBLIGATION TO BUY...NOW OR EVER!

GUARANTEED

PLAY "ROLL A DOUBLE" AND GET AS MANY AS SIX GIFTS!

HERE'S HOW TO PLAY:

1. Peel off label from front cover. Place it in space provided at right. With a coin, carefully scratch off the silver dice. This makes you eligible to receive one or more free books, and possibly other gifts, depending on what is revealed beneath the scratch-off area.

2. You'll receive brand-new Harlequin Presents® novels. When you return this card, we'll rush you the books and gifts you qualify for ABSOLUTELY FREE!

3. Then, if we don't hear from you, every month we'll send you 6 additional novels to read and enjoy. You can return them and owe nothing, but if you decide to keep them, you'll pay only $2.24* per book-a savings of 26¢ each off the cover price.

4. When you subscribe to the Harlequin Reader Service®, you'll also get our newsletter, as well as additional free gifts from time to time.

5. You must be completely satisfied. You may cancel at any time simply by sending us a note or a shipping statement marked "cancel" or by returning any shipment to us at our expense.

You'll love your elegant 20K gold electroplated chain! The necklace is finely crafted with 160 double- soldered links, and is electroplate finished in genuine 20K gold. And it's yours FREE as an added thanks for giving our Reader Service a try!

"ROLL A DOUBLE!"

PLACE LABEL HERE

SCRATCH HERE

SEE CLAIM CHART BELOW

106 CIH BA6G
(U-H-P-09/90)

YES! I have placed my label from the front cover into the space provided above and scratched off the silver dice. Please rush me the free book(s) and gift(s) that I am entitled to. I understand that I am under no obligation to purchase any books, as explained on the opposite page.

NAME

ADDRESS   APT.

CITY   STATE   ZIP CODE

CLAIM CHART

	4 FREE BOOKS PLUS FREE 20k ELECTROPLATED GOLD CHAIN PLUS MYSTERY BONUS GIFT
	3 FREE BOOKS PLUS BONUS GIFT
	2 FREE BOOKS

CLAIM NO.37-829

BUSINESS REPLY MAIL

FIRST CLASS MAIL   PERMIT NO. 717   BUFFALO, NY

POSTAGE WILL BE PAID BY ADDRESSEE

HARLEQUIN READER SERVICE
PO BOX 1867
BUFFALO NY 14240-9952

NO POSTAGE
NECESSARY
IF MAILED
IN THE
UNITED STATES

He closed his eyes and she went to stand by the window. She was wondering how soon she could push him out of the room, when she heard the sound of a snore. Dammit! He'd fallen asleep. He had unbuttoned his shirt and taken off his jacket in the bathroom, and not bothered to put it on again. It made him look less obnoxious, and for the first time she saw the humour of the situation. But humour or not, he couldn't remain here, and she shook him by the shoulder. A louder snore was his only answer, and she debated whether to call Milly or Peter. But it was childish to panic. Larry, in this state, was no threat, and would be annoyed if she asked someone to carry him off. Better try to rouse him in a little while.

An hour passed before she succeeded, and with grunts and groans he surfaced to consciousness.

'I hope I haven't blotted my copybook?' he apologised, his jacket over his arm as he stood up.

'It happens to the best of us,' she said. 'I'm glad you're feeling better.'

'You're a great girl.' His prominent eyes were no longer tinged with lust. 'If you want to be the "Rowena Girl", the job's yours. I'll have a word with Mrs Pearce.'

He stepped into the corridor, then reached out and drew her to him. She tensed, knowing that if he tried anything on she would hit him regardless. But to her relief he merely kissed her cheek.

'You're a great girl,' he repeated. 'Be seeing you.'

Not if I see you first, Lorraine thought as she locked the door behind him. Yet why worry about Larry when there were many other things to disturb her? No, not many. Only one. A man called Jason. He had said he loved her, yet his actions didn't always speak it, and they definitely hadn't done so tonight. Not for the first time, she wondered whether love, to him, was simply desire.

Until she knew exactly where she stood with him, how he saw her in his life, whether in fact he *did* see her in his life, she would have no peace.

CHAPTER NINE

THE HOUSE was empty when Lorraine entered it mid-morning the following day. A note from Margaret on the hall table informed her that, since school had broken up for the summer vacation, she had taken Paul and Jilly to the Zoo in Regent's Park.

Unable to settle to anything, Lorraine strolled into the garden to pick some flowers. Instinctively her eyes wandered next door, but the house appeared deserted: windows closed, curtains drawn. She couldn't wait to see Jason, and rehearsed exactly what to say to him. If only he'd return soon so she could get it over with!

She was in the middle of a salad lunch when Denis telephoned, and, even as he enquired how she was, his intonation warned her that something was wrong.

'Give it to me straight,' she declared. 'I can take it.'

But it was far worse than she had anticipated. The Stanways had apparently been having her watched, and a private detective had photographs of Larry Pethco leaving her room at the Metropole at two o'clock this morning. Because of this they were demanding immediate custody of the children.

'You're single and a free agent,' Denis went on, 'but quite honestly, I'm astonished you weren't more circumspect.'

'Larry isn't my lover and I've never had one!' she exploded, and angrily explained how he had come to

be in her room. 'So you can tell His Lordship he hasn't
a hope of taking Paul and Jilly away from me.'

'It isn't as easy as that, I'm afraid. I believe you,
but I doubt anyone else will.'

'Larry will endorse what I've said.'

'Don't be naïve, Lorraine. The Stanways will argue
that it's the man's way of sliding out of an awkward
situation.'

'But it's the truth! Look, Denis, I won't give up
the children without a fight, and if——'

'You'll lose—those photographs make it a fore-
gone conclusion. If you were married with a secure
home, it would be a different story.'

'Then I'll find a husband!' Lorraine fired back.

'Do that, and we'll re-apply for custody.'

'You mean I have to give them up *now*, this
minute?'

'Not this minute,' Denis said sympathetically, 'but
within the next day or so.'

Sick at heart, Lorraine ended the conversation, and
was brooding wretchedly over the news when she
heard a step on the front path. The knowledge that
it might be Jason did little to untie the knot in her
stomach, and with leaden legs she opened the front
door, resisting the urge to slam it shut when she found
herself confronting Erica.

'What do you want?' she demanded.

'I came to see Jason, but he isn't home yet. And
it's too hot to wait in the car.'

'He has a front lawn,' Lorraine said, then, realising
she was being gratuitously rude—after all, Erica
hadn't done her any harm—she mumbled an apology
and stepped aside.

'Sorry I'm in such a foul mood, but I've had bad news.'

'About your nephew and niece?'

'Yes. Who told you?'

'I guessed.' Erica moistened her lips. 'Any chance of a cool drink?'

'Of course.' Lorraine went into the kitchen and Erica followed.

'I can't think why Jason's late,' the girl went on. 'He promised to be here by one-thirty.'

'Do you crack the whip so hard over all your authors?' Lorraine asked drily.

'I wasn't cracking the whip last night,' said Erica. 'That was purely social. He was visiting his uncle and I was staying overnight with my parents. I told you we're neighbours—since Jason was fourteen, in fact.'

Lorraine handed the girl a tonic water with ice. 'I didn't realise he'd lived with his uncle as a boy.'

'Oh, yes. His father died when he was eight, and when his mother married a Spaniard and moved to Barcelona, she decided it was best Jason remain in England.'

'Strange,' commented Lorraine.

'Not really. He's heir to the title and Lord Sta——' Erica stopped abruptly, her face red.

Lorraine's was red too—the red of anger as her intelligence told her that the name Erica hadn't finished saying was 'Stanway'.

How could she have been so stupid as to believe Jason had rented the house next door because his apartment didn't give him the peace and quiet he wanted? The swine had moved here to spy on her! The Stanways hadn't hired a private detective—they'd used Jason!

'I—I'm awfully sorry,' Erica stammered. 'I didn't mean to tell you.'

'Yes, you did! That's why you came here.'

Erica's colour flared again. 'You're right. To be honest, I found I didn't like Jason making a fool of you.'

'How touching! I'd no idea you were such a feminist. I assume you've also heard about the photographs?'

'Yes, and I must admit they surprised me. Jason was shattered when the detective delivered them to the Stanways this morning.'

Lorraine swallowed hard. 'You mean I've had Jason *and* a private eye watching me?'

Erica nodded. 'Jason didn't learn about the other man until today. Apparently his uncle engaged him as a back-up.'

'Why?'

'Because Jason's always been a push-over for a pretty face, and Lord Stanway thought... Well, you can guess.'

'Too well,' Lorraine said crisply, wondering what plan Jason would have dreamed up to discredit her if the detective hadn't beaten him to it.

'You've fallen for him, haven't you?' Erica stated bluntly.

This was an honesty Lorraine couldn't tolerate. 'Your wires are crossed on that one,' she said, with just the right amount of amusement. 'He's marvellous company, and he helped me at a period in my life when I was finding it hard to cope. But I certainly don't love him, though I grant you he's fanciable!'

At this, Erica laughed. 'I'd love to watch Jason's face when he hears that!'

Lorraine forced indifference to the remark. 'I don't want to turf you out,' she said lightly, 'but I've several calls to make.'

'Of course.' Erica set down her glass. 'Will you tell Jason I told you he's Lord Stanway's nephew, or will you pretend you've known all along?'

This was a suggestion Lorraine hadn't considered.

'It will save your pride,' the girl continued. 'And I always think that's important for a woman.'

As if Erica cared a fig about saving anyone's face other than her own! 'Scared Jason will be angry with you for giving him away?' Lorraine asked forthrightly.

'Partly. Though I'm sure he had no intention of carrying on with the charade once the lawyers had the photographs. I mean, he hasn't any reason to now, has he?'

Lorraine ignored the question, concentrating instead on what to do. Erica's suggestion wasn't to be dismissed, for if she had to visit the Stanways to see Paul and Jilly, she was bound to bump into Jason there. And she'd do anything in the world to prevent him discovering what a fool he'd made of her.

'Very well,' she said aloud. 'I won't tell Jason you were here. That way we'll both have what we want.'

Smiling happily, Erica left; alone again, Lorraine felt she had hit rock bottom once more. Losing her parents and then her brother had been two bitter blows, but to discover Jason's duplicity and also to lose Paul and Jilly... Tears poured down her cheeks. Things she had believed had proved false, people she had trusted had turned out untrustworthy. It was a chilling thought, and she felt as if she was surrounded by enemies.

'I suppose Margaret knew who Jason was?' she called out through the open window.

'Oh, yes.' Erica stopped by the gate. 'But Jason genuinely wanted to bring her in to help you. And don't be upset with Margaret. Only the other day she told Jason she was going to tell you the truth, but he begged her to hold off a while longer.'

Now she wouldn't need to, Lorraine thought, turning away, and wished she could as easily turn away from the world.

Yet this was impossible. The truth, no matter how ugly, had to be faced, and she would have to make Jason believe that, far from his fooling her, she had been fooling him!

She paced the room, carefully working out what to say. She had to pretend she had known all along about his relationship with Lord Stanway. But would he believe her? She had to make sure he did, for only then could she rescue her pride and make her life bearable.

Lorraine was still planning what to say to Jason when she heard steps coming up the front path. Heart racing, she hurried to peer at herself in the mirror. Luckily her face did not reflect her anguish, and, drawing a deep breath, she opened the door.

Blankly she stared at the tall, fair-haired man on the threshold. A door-to-door salesman? A private detective to collect the children?

'Yes?' she questioned. 'What do you want?'

'You!'

Annoyed, she went to close the door, but a large foot prevented her. Frightened out of her wits, she pushed harder. Jason was always warning her to keep the chain on, but fool that she was she'd ignored him.

'Don't you recognise me?' the voice asked. 'When we last spoke I told you I was coming back from Australia.'

'James!' she screamed, and flung the door wide, bursting into tears as she fell into his arms.

He held her close, words superfluous as they each knew the other was thinking of Edward and how tragically his life had been cut short. Except that her tears weren't only for her brother; they were for his children, whom she had lost, and for Jason, whom she had never had.

'Sorry for making a fool of myself,' she murmured at last, leading him inside. 'But seeing you again after all this time brought back memories.'

'For me, too.' James's voice was as calm and English as she remembered it, though in other respects he appeared different.

'I'm sorry I didn't recognise you,' she apologised. 'You've changed.'

'It's only been six years.'

'Maybe, but you're thinner and blonder and younger-looking.'

'What balm to thirty-four-year-old ears!' he chuckled. 'But you've changed too. When I went away you were a lovely young girl; now you're a beautiful woman.'

Well, one thing had remained the same, Lorraine thought, dismayed, as she led him into the sitting-room.

He looked around him. 'I thought the children were with you?'

'They are, but they're spending the day at the Zoo.'

'Do you see anything of Denis and Sally?'

'Quite a bit. Denis is acting for me.'

'Why? You have problems?'

Briefly she recounted them, telling him of Jason's duplicity but careful to omit that she had fallen in love with him.

'It now looks as if the Stanways will get what they want,' she concluded. 'At least until I marry.'

'*I'm* available,' James said promptly.

She knew he meant it, but pretended otherwise. 'Sweet of you,' she said easily, 'but that would be stretching your friendship too far.'

'Don't be so sure.'

She didn't answer and he seemed happy to drop the subject. A subtle man, James, she decided, surreptitiously appraising him, and a stronger character than she recollected. Either that, or teenage eyes hadn't seen beyond the matinee idol looks.

He was far more handsome today; his brown eyes humorous, his skin surprisingly unlined, given that he had been subjected for so many years to the bright Australian sunshine. His rather wide mouth was curved with good nature, and his blond hair was well-cut but tousled, as if he constantly ran his fingers through it. He was not as tall as she remembered, being about five foot ten, but he was strongly built and moved with an easy stride. An exceptionally attractive man, provided one didn't compare him with— hastily Lorraine controlled her errant thoughts.

For the next hour they brought each other up to date on their lives, and only at the end did James comment on Jason.

'What an underhand swine he was, to hide his identity! I can understand that he wanted to help his family, but to do it in such a way...' James paused, then said carefully, 'Mind you, I feel you weren't

thinking clearly when you decided to saddle yourself
with two kids, especially when they have willing and
able grandparents.'

'If they hadn't treated Edward and Anne so harshly,
I——'

'Forget all that. People change, my dear, and from
what you've said, they obviously regret their
behaviour.'

Recollecting Lord Stanway's rudeness to her,
Lorraine couldn't agree, but deemed it wiser not to
argue. The situation had been resolved—for the
moment—and to keep her temper at boiling point over
it was unwise. Until she was in a position to fight for
the children, it was less wearing emotionally to accept
the situation.

'When are you leaving for New York?' James
enquired.

'I'm not sure. I may stop here if I can get enough
work.'

'I hope you do,' came the fervent response. 'I'll be
here for eighteen months and it will give us a chance
to know each other.'

'We've know each other since I was ten!'

'That's not quite the same!'

She eyed him affectionately, aware that with this
man she would be secure, and wishing it were possible
to love to order.

'I'd best be heading for my pad,' he announced.
'I'll meet the kids another time.'

'I'm not sure when they'll be leaving me.' Her lips
trembled and he put a reassuring hand on her arm.

'Are you free to have dinner with me on Friday
night?'

'I won't feel like it if the children have just gone.'

'All the more reason to go out. Moping won't help.'

Lorraine sighed her agreement. 'As long as you're prepared for a weepy female.'

'I'll bring an extra handkerchief with me! I'll call you on Friday to fix a time.'

She went with him to his car, comforted by the warmth of his arm across her shoulders.

'Call me if you need me, Lorraine,' he said. 'You know how I felt about Edward, and if there's anything I can do to help...'

Turning her to face him, he encircled her with his arms. His strength and gentleness were what she needed, and she rested against him, feeling her tension ebb.

'Sweet girl,' he muttered, tilting her head to find her lips.

She let him kiss her, though she was unable to respond. He seemed unaware of it, for his mouth firmed and pressed harder, and only the sound of an approaching car made him pull back. As he did, Lorraine saw Jason step out of his Porsche, fling her a look of contempt and stride past her into his house.

'The nephew, I take it?' said James.

'Yes.' Lorraine couldn't wait for James to go, and even as she returned to the house she saw Jason come in through the back door.

'Sorry I broke up the love scene,' he drawled.

'You didn't. James was leaving.'

'Another boyfriend?'

'Another?' she echoed, looking innocent, then allowed understanding to cross her face. 'Oh, of course. Those snaps of Larry coming out of my room this morning. How you and your uncle must have gloated over them!'

The realisation that she knew his identity was a shock Jason couldn't hide. 'When did you find out?' he asked quietly.

'About the photographs, or *you*?'

'Both.'

'I learned about the photos when Denis called me this morning and advised me not to fight your uncle for the children. As for *your* identity...' she gave a slight smile, 'I suspected it from day one.'

'How could you have?'

Aware that he disbelieved her—and with good reason, for she'd been completely fooled—she knew she had to lie with bravado.

'When your last book came out, I read an article about you in a magazine in the States. Among other things, it said you were heir to Lord Stanway.'

'I don't believe you. Only a handful of people are aware of my relationship to him, and no article's ever appeared about it.'

'Sounds as if your press cutting agency isn't doing its job,' she shrugged. '*Uncover* specialises in disclosure stories, and that's where I read it.' Devoutly she hoped he wouldn't contact the magazine to find out if she was lying. 'You put on a good act, Jason, but it was a waste.'

'You put on a good act yourself,' he replied. 'You fooled *me* completely. But why did you let me carry on the pretence?'

This was the question she had been waiting for, and she took her time delivering the blow to his ego.

'I figured you'd be more likely to plead my cause with your uncle if you fell for me. I wasn't sure whether to succumb to your charms immediately, or make you wait, but I finally decided you'd respect me more if I played Miss Innocent.' She widened her eyes at him. 'I wasn't wrong, was I? If it hadn't been for those photos, you'd still be trying to seduce me. And once we were lovers, I could have had some influence over you.'

Tensely she waited for his reaction. If Jason admitted he'd genuinely grown to care for her, she'd cast pride to the wind and come clean. Even if he simply showed regret for what had occurred, she'd be honest with him. But he did neither.

Instead he laughed. A deep, rollicking laugh.

'Sorry to disappoint you, my sweet, but your charms—undeniable though they are—would never have dissuaded me from what I set out to do—which was to prove you morally unsuitable to have control of my two young cousins. It was a stroke of luck that Pethco came on the scene and saved me from making the supreme sacrifice!' Grey eyes gleamed mockingly. 'Not too big a sacrifice, actually. You're an extremely beddable female.'

Every word he spoke was like a dagger in her heart, the pain so intense that Lorraine was incapable of speaking. Incredibly, Jason saw her lack of response as indifference, and turned away from her with a mutter of contempt.

'Make sure Paul and Jilly are ready to leave with me in the morning,' he said. 'I'm taking them to Stanway Hall myself.'

'This isn't the end of the story,' she retorted with equal contempt. 'Only a hiatus.'

Without replying, he left her.

Lorraine was still numb with shock when Margaret returned with the children. They fell upon her as though she had been away a month rather than twenty-four hours, and, conscious that this was her last night with them for a long time to come, she could hardly bear to let them go to bed.

Inevitably tiredness made it a necessity, but even when they were asleep she sat in a chair beside them, staring into their innocent faces and letting the tears course unchecked down her cheeks.

They still glittered wetly when she walked into the kitchen and woodenly told Margaret the children were going to their grandparents next day.

The older woman flushed. 'I've been wanting to——'

'I know all about it,' Lorraine interjected, and Margaret coloured deeply.

'I felt so guilty deceiving you, but when Mr Fletcher begged me to help out, I——'

'Forget it. I'm not angry with you. I just hope you'll stay with the children. Then they'll at least have a familiar face around them.'

'Of course I'll stay,' Margaret said at once, then added in a rush, 'I can't believe Lord Stanway thinks they'll be better off with him, when they love you so. I'm astonished Mr Fletcher hasn't tried to change his uncle's mind.'

'Why should he?' Lorraine said tonelessly. 'He agrees with him.'

Next morning she told Paul and Jilly they would be going to their grandparents for a while, and, though tearful at the news, they cheered up when they heard Margaret was accompanying them.

'Why can't you come too?' Paul enquired.

'I'll be down to see you, but my home is here.'

'This is my home as well,' Paul said sturdily. 'And Jilly's. Mummy and Daddy lived here.'

Lorraine swallowed the lump in her throat. 'Your mummy also lived in the house where you're going. It's very old and I'm sure it has lots of secret rooms you can explore.'

'How will we get to school?' he asked, ever practical.

'You'll be going to a new one and making many new friends.'

'Don't you want us any more?' he demanded bluntly.

This was almost Lorraine's undoing, and she knelt and hugged them both. 'I'll always want you, my darlings, but for the moment I can't have you.'

Pride gave her the strength to watch calmly as Jason arrived to collect the cases. They greeted each other with cool civility, which she maintained as she sauntered down the path and watched her nephew and niece clamber into the car. By keeping her mind blank she was also able to remain by the gate, smiling and waving till the Porsche was out of sight.

Even then her contempt for Jason acted as a brake on her grief. All she felt was determination. One day she would obtain custody of the children, make Jason regret the devious game he had played with her heart, and hurt him as he had hurt her.

CHAPTER TEN

SITTING in the restaurant with James on Friday night, listening to a trio playing 'What Is This Thing Called Love?', Lorraine wondered if she was the only person here seriously considering the answer to that question.

And not finding one either. Perhaps there *was* no answer! Or maybe every person had a different one. Personally, she knew love wasn't logical. How could it be, when she could continue loving a man she despised?

These past few days had been a nightmare of loneliness, but James had been a tower of strength. He had called her every day, sometimes twice, and when she had asked for a rain check on their date tonight, had insisted that once she was out with him she'd feel better.

'By next week you'll be ready to face the future,' he said now, breaking into her thoughts.

'That's what I keep telling myself,' she sighed, 'but I guess I'm deaf to reason.'

'Like most women!' he teased, then grew serious again. 'You're not as alone as you think, Lorraine. You always have me.'

'I know, and I'm very grateful. I owe Fate a great thank-you for sending you over from Australia.'

'I'll remember to tell her.'

'It might be a him!'

'Impossible. Fate's illogical and capricious—it has to be a her!'

Lorraine laughed and, pleased that he had cheered her, James set out to retain the mood, regaling her with a fund of stories about his acting career.

If only he appealed to her, she thought as he drove her home later that evening; yet, though they had a past in common, she couldn't visualise a future with him.

'I'm motoring down to Wiltshire to visit some cousins tomorrow,' he said. 'Care to join me?'

'I'm meeting Sally and Denis,' she told him.

'Sunday, then? If the weather holds, we can go to the coast.'

'Sunday's out too, I'm afraid. Cindy—a girlfriend of mine from the States—is flying in.'

'Let's make it the evening, then.'

Lorraine couldn't help chuckling. 'Are you always so persistent?'

'When I want something badly.'

'Not *me*, James. I don't want to hurt you.'

'I'm glad to hear it.'

'Be serious!' she begged.

'I am. Serious enough to bide my time. So we won't talk about it.' He paused, then resumed on an entirely different tack. 'I'm starting rehearsals Monday and want to practise my lines. I generally use a tape recorder to feed me, but it would be great if you did it.'

'Me?' But I'm a rotten actress.'

'No acting's required. You simply read me Marlene's lines. She's the woman I plan to marry once I've murdered my wife!'

'Great! And here I was, thinking you were the hero!'

'Women find villains more interesting.' James' tone was so dry that Lorraine wondered if he had guessed her real feelings for Jason.

If he had, he deemed it wiser not to say so, and for the rest of the drive discussed his part in the series.

Saturday was thoroughly miserable for her. It was her first one away from the children, and seeing Sally and Denis with their two increased her misery.

On Sunday morning she decided to speak to Margaret, pretty sure the Stanways would be at church. She was right, and Paul had gone with them, though Jilly was home with a cold.

'They're settling down very well,' Margaret assured her. 'They have a swing and climbing frame in the garden, masses of games and toys, and of course the dogs. Goldie—Lady Stanway's retriever—had pups three months ago and the children have chosen one each. They're besotted with them.'

Lorraine could well believe it. 'Do you think it will upset Jilly if she spoke to me?'

'Not at all. She's just come into the room and I'll hand you over to her.'

Lorraine was soon being regaled with everything Jilly had done and been given, though it seemed that the highlight was Jason's visit that day.

'He's coming to lunch and then taking us somewhere special,' Jilly babbled on. 'Will you be coming, too?'

'I'm afraid not, darling.'

'When can we come home?'

'I'm not sure. But you can always talk to me. Just ask Margaret to ring me.'

'Seeing you is nicer than talking.'

Lorraine couldn't help smiling at Jilly's quick response, and was filled with such bitterness against the Stanways that she hurriedly ended the call.

Anxious to leave the house, she showered and changed into a lemon silk dress and matching silk-knit cardigan. She wasn't meeting Cindy till lunchtime, but she parked the car in Regent's Park and went for a stroll until it was time to make her way to the Connaught.

She had been delighted when Cindy had called to say she'd be in London for a day, and Lorraine had wondered whether it was for a TV commercial or a photo session. Either way, the clients were extremely generous, she thought now as her friend met her at the door of an elegant suite. Either detergent or dog food. They were always the most lavish spenders.

Cindy was no less elegant than her surroundings. Tall and thin, she normally favoured dramatic colours and outlandish styles, but today was a Gainsborough girl in a cascade of lilac silk. Even her hair, black as a seal and usually worn in a dramatic short bob, followed her new image and was longer and softly waved.

'It's great seeing you!' Cindy exclaimed, hugging her.

'Same here. How long are you staying, and who's the client?'

'I'm leaving later this afternoon, and the client's Dexter Blake the Third.'

'Is it detergent or dog food?' Lorraine asked.

'It's marriage!' Cindy declared dramatically, extending a scarlet-tipped hand to show a knuckle-duster of a diamond ring.

Lorraine gaped at it, then hugged her friend again. 'Why didn't you phone and tell me about it? How long have you known him? What's he like? When did it happen?'

'Hey, one question at a time! It happened the night before I phoned you, and I've known him since I was six, though he's only known *me* two months.'

'That's as clear as mud. Explain yourself.'

'Well, Dex and I grew up in the same small town, but he was rich rich and I was poor poor. Which meant I knew all about *him*, but he knew nothing of me. Until a month ago, that is, when he came to New York to sign some business deal or other and was taken to a party at the Plaza.'

'Where he met you and asked where you'd been all his life,' Lorraine prompted.

'As near as makes no difference,' Cindy agreed. 'And I said I'd been right under his nose for years!'

'He seems to have made up for lost time,' said Lorraine, admiring the ring once more.

'It was love at first sight.' Cindy's small, heart-shaped face grew serious. 'I'd always had a crush on Dex, and I still can't believe my luck.'

'*He's* lucky too,' Lorraine said staunchly, aware that behind her friend's glamorous front was a warm and lovely person. 'Where's Dex now? I'd like to meet him.'

'Not this trip. He flew directly to Paris for a meeting, but I insisted on stopping over in London to meet you. I'd planned on being here overnight, but he's missing me so dreadfully, he called and begged me to join him this evening.'

'A plea you can't refuse,' Lorraine added solemnly.

'I can't refuse that guy anything. He's the greatest thing that's walked into my life.' Big brown eyes glowed with joy. 'Hey, come to Paris with me. I'll be there all week, and we can go shopping and——'

'I'm busy organising my career,' Lorraine cut in. 'And going out of town at this stage won't help it any.'

Instantly Cindy sobered. 'Fill me in on the latest details.'

Though Lorraine was unwilling to mar her friend's happiness with her own saga of woe, Cindy would have none of it, and over a delicious lunch in the Grill Room insisted on being brought up to date.

'I'll never read another Jason Fletcher book in my life!' she declared. 'What a two-faced, rotten...' Words failed her and she downed her coffee at a gulp.

'I don't blame him for hiding his identity,' Lorraine felt obliged to say. 'It's pretending he loved me that really hurts. Not that he actually spoke of a future together, but...'

'But he was ready to go to bed with you, though he damn well knew you weren't the sort of person who'd do *that* lightly! So don't bother defending him, honey. He's a rat!'

'That's what I keep reminding myself, but I still can't get over him.' Determinedly Lorraine changed the subject. 'No more of Jason. It's a lovely afternoon and how do you want to spend it?'

'Will you think me a hick if I suggest the waxworks?'

Lorraine's eyebrows rose. 'Madame Tussauds?'

'Right. It's as near as I'm ever going to be to your Royals!'

Lorraine burst out laughing. 'It will be crowded as a bees' nest,' she explained, 'but if you don't mind it...'

'I'll love it.'

Lorraine reminded her of this as they stood in the long queue waiting to enter, but neither the heat nor the jostling crowds could dim Cindy's enthusiasm.

'Imagine what it must feel like to stare back at yourself,' Cindy mused before a replica of Princess Di.

'I do it every time I look in the mirror!' Lorraine teased. 'Now stop gawping at Her Royal Highness and I'll fill you in on our history.'

Dredging up all she knew of the famous and infamous figures on display, Lorraine found herself enjoying the waxworks more than she had expected. If only she'd thought to bring the children here! Paul would have loved the battle scenes, which were highlighted by music and gunfire, and Jilly would have adored Sleeping Beauty.

But wasn't that her nephew and niece ahead of her? She shook her head and closed her eyes. If she didn't stop thinking about them, she'd start imagining them everywhere! Opening her eyes, she found them still there, on the far side of the room, and knew it wasn't her imagination, but reality. To make it more gut-wrenching, they were with Jason!

He was completely absorbed in them, one hand on Paul's shoulder, the other clasped by Jilly's. Lorraine feasted her eyes on his profile, drinking in every line of it: the slightly long nose, the high cheekbone tapering to the firm chin, the wide forehead and the careless fall of black hair she ached to touch.

She held her breath, waiting for Erica to appear, but there was no sign of her. Just this grey-suited Adonis with the two children.

The three of them turned and began walking in her direction, though she knew they hadn't noticed her. For a split second she considered jumping on one of the stands and pretending to be a waxwork herself, but knew she would never pull it off.

'There's Lorri!' Paul suddenly shouted, and dashed across to her.

Jilly was fast on his heels, and Lorraine bent to cuddle them. Inevitably Jason joined them and she mumbled introductions to Cindy, glad that her friend, as if guessing her state of mind, hogged the conversation and kept him occupied.

'Will you have tea with us, Lorri?' asked Paul, his pointed little face still flushed with the pleasure of seeing her.

'I'm afraid we can't, darling. Cindy and I are busy.'

'Surely not too busy for a quick cuppa!' Jason's deep voice was faintly amused, as though seeing through her subterfuge.

'We really *are* busy,' Cindy interpolated prettily. 'I'm off to Paris later this afternoon, and Lorraine's driving me to the airport.'

'In that case, we won't keep you.' He tapped Jilly's curls. 'Hurry up, Miss Monster, before all the ice-cream is eaten.'

Even the prospect of ice-cream couldn't come between Jilly and her love for her aunt, and she flung herself into Lorraine's arms and burst into tears. 'I don't want to leave you. I want to go home with you.'

'Soon, sweetheart,' Lorraine promised. 'But you have to be with your grandparents a little longer.'

'I've already told Jilly that,' Paul said loftily, 'but she's too little to remember.'

'I'se not little!' Jilly cried.

'Come on, you two,' Jason ordered, his eyes cold as ice as they flickered over Lorraine.

Not waiting to see if the children obeyed him, Lorraine caught Cindy's arm and propelled her from the room.

'What a rotten end to a lovely afternoon,' her friend commented.

'But at least I got to meet the famous Jason Fletcher. I can understand why you fell for him.' She paused dramatically. 'And he's not unmoved by *you*.'

'I didn't say he was. He fancied me, and thought he'd try his luck.'

'Which puts him on a par with most men,' Cindy retorted. 'But you've got under his skin, honey. I saw the way he was eyeing you. Pity you didn't meet in normal circumstances.'

'In normal circumstances our paths wouldn't have crossed,' Lorraine said with irony. 'Anyway, Jason's expedient, and will only love where it suits him.'

'I won't argue on that score. You know him better than I do. But where *your* happiness is concerned I'm ready to give advice. So move back to New York and forget the whole thing.'

'I refuse to give up the children.'

'No one's asking you to. But your brother wouldn't have wanted you to make your life miserable because of them, which is precisely what you're doing.'

Cindy would have expounded on the subject had time not been rushing by and her flight to Paris imminent, for which Lorraine was grateful. Well-meaning though friends were, there came a time when the best advice in the world was unacceptable, and you had to do what your heart dictated, though you knew it to be illogical.

CHAPTER ELEVEN

LORRAINE was grateful she had agreed to see James that evening, and his arrival, with a large manuscript and a bottle of wine, helped restore her spirits.

'Had a good afternoon?' he asked, kissing her lightly on the lips and settling back in an armchair with the whisky she brought him.

'Yes,' she replied, then told him of her encounter with Jason.

'How did you feel about it?'

Uncertain whether he was referring to the children or Jason, she shrugged his question aside, glad when he took the hint and held out the manuscript to her.

'I've brought along the first episode,' he said.

'Shall we run through it?'

'Let's eat first—I'm starving. Need any help?'

'No, thanks, I'm cooking with a can-opener! Relax with the Sunday papers.'

During supper they chatted easily, and Lorraine felt she and James were back where they had left off, when he'd been climbing the ladder of success and she'd been a sixteen-year-old, unsure what to do with her life. She wasn't all that sure now, she admitted to him as he helped her clear the dishes.

'Follow your instincts,' he advised.

This was exactly what she had told herself a few hours ago when she had been irritated by Cindy's suggestions. Yet now she was doubtful.

'The trouble is, I keep changing my mind,' she said aloud. 'Of course, if I'm lucky I can have as good a career here as in the States.'

'In that case, live where you'll be happiest.' James's arm around her shoulders, they went into the sitting-room. 'If you're ready, Sarah Bernhardt, let's get started!'

They did a fast run through the episode he had brought, and Lorraine found it fun to act the part he had marked out for her.

'You're doing it damn well!' he exclaimed at the end of their first long scene. 'If you ever decide to change professions, let me know. With your looks you could——'

'Play a blonde bimbo?' She laughed. 'No, James, if I'm reading it well, it's only because I'm not embarrassed with you. But put me in front of a camera and I'd freeze.'

'You don't freeze doing a commercial.'

'That's different.'

He let her answer go, preparing for the morrow being more important than discussing a change in her career.

Inevitably they came to a love scene, and, aware that his feelings for her could be aroused all too easily, Lorraine fed him her lines in her most matter-of-fact voice.

Not so James, who flung himself into his part as if the camera was whirring.

'"I'll let no one stand between us!"' he thundered. '"My money means nothing to me if I can't share it with you. I never knew love could be like this, and I'll do everything in my power to make you love me."'

'"You won't have to try very hard,"' she read. '"I love you already, darling. How blind you are not to see it!"'

'"Do you really mean it?"' He flung out an arm.

'"Don't you know I do?"' The scene was so dramatic it was hard to keep her voice flat. '"Of course I mean it. You're everything I've ever wanted and never dreamed I'd find. Oh, how I love you! If only——"' Abruptly she stopped. 'What was that?'

'What?' Frowning, James came back to the present.

'I thought I heard a sound.'

He went to the window and peered out. 'I can't see anyone. It was probably a neighbour.' He returned to the centre of the room. 'Mind if we go through the whole thing again?'

'I'm rather tired,' she apologised.

In fact she was exhausted. Confiding her troubles to Cindy had brought back all the pain, and encountering Jason had made it worse.

'I know it isn't late,' she added, 'but I've been sleeping badly and——'

'No sweat. You've been wonderful.' James picked up the play. 'I'll be rehearsing all week and I'm not sure what time we break at night.'

'Call me when you can,' she said easily. 'If I'm not working, I'll see you.'

'I'd like to see you every night.' His voice was suffused with gentleness. 'The words I said to you a while ago weren't acting. I meant them.'

'Oh, James,' she said softly, 'I'm not ready for love.'

'I told you I'm patient,' he murmured.

'Don't be. It won't do you any good.'

'Is there someone else?'

She wanted to lie, but knew it wouldn't be fair to him. 'Yes,' she nodded. 'But he—he isn't free.'

James scanned her face, his own reflective. 'I'm a patient man,' he reiterated. 'Remember that.'

Locking the door after her, Lorraine returned to the kitchen and emptied the dishwasher—a homely task to remind her that no matter how one felt, life went on. The dishes put away, she wiped the kitchen table and resisted the urge to scrub the floor. If she went on like this, she'd have the most pristine house in the neighbourhood!

A rap on the window-pane almost frightened her out of her skin, and she darted towards the telephone, stopping as she heard her name called.

'Jason!' she said fiercely, and opened the back door to him. 'You gave me one hell of a fright!'

'Sorry.' He sounded completely indifferent. 'I dropped in to give you these.'

'These' were two coloured drawings: one of a large house, half hidden by trees, the other of ducks on a lake.

'From the children,' she murmured.

'Yes.' Jason's voice was brittle. 'When I told them I was bringing them to London, they asked to drop these in on you. I'd actually planned on doing so after we'd had tea.'

'Why didn't you give them to me this afternoon?'

'They were in the car, and you rushed off before I could fetch them.'

'I'm sorry you had to come all the way out here,' she said stiltedly. 'You should have posted them.'

'I was coming here anyway to collect my things.'

'Of course. Living next door has served its purpose now you have what you want.'

'Too true. And you seem to be getting what *you* want.'

'I beg your pardon?'

'A rich man falling over himself to marry you. Do you really love him, Lorraine, or are you using his money to help you get the children back?'

Astounded, she stared at him. It must have been Jason she had heard outside the window a while ago and, overhearing her rehearse with James, he had taken it for real!

She was on the verge of scornfully saying he was misjudging her yet again, when she changed her mind. *Let* him think James was a millionaire who wanted to marry her!

'What a great actress you'd make,' Jason went on, his sensuous mouth a slit of derision. 'First you fooled me, and now you're fooling this other sucker.'

'All in a good cause,' she said brightly. 'I'll do everything in my power to have Paul and Jilly.'

'If you genuinely care about their happiness, you'll leave them where they are,' he said flatly. 'They need a stable home life.'

'They'll have it with me.'

'For how long? Till your millionaire wakes up to the fact that you used him? You know, I almost feel sorry for the poor devil. First me, then Pethco, and now him!'

Lorraine caught her breath. Jason had hurt her before, but nothing like he was hurting her now. She closed her eyes, calling on her innermost resources to hide her pain.

'You don't count,' she said quietly. 'Don't forget I'd discovered who you were and deliberately set out to make you fall for me.'

'Ah, yes,' he mocked. 'By offering me your body. Is it still on offer, I wonder?'

Too late she realised his intention, and as she went to rush past him, he pulled her back and swung her into his arms.

'No, you don't,' he said thickly, and pressed his mouth so savagely upon her own that her lips were forced back. His teeth ground against her gums and she tasted blood. How dared he use brute strength to overcome her? She struggled in his arms, but was as powerless as a butterfly pinned down. And to emphasise his victory he drove his tongue between her teeth.

At the feel of its warmth, Lorraine shivered and gasped, the movement giving him triumphant entrance, so that he penetrated the moist depths to the full, exploring the soft cavern until there was no part of it left untouched.

It was a kiss of such intimacy, it was hard to believe it was done uncaringly, and she was overwhelmed with sadness that what should have been wonderful should leave her feeling degraded. Once more she struggled to be free, and he laughed deep in his throat and pushed her back on the settee. She felt herself falling, falling, until she was flat on the cushions and Jason was on top of her, his body pressing her into the soft depths.

She pummelled at his chest, but he clasped her flailing hands and adroitly pinned them behind her.

'Give in and enjoy it,' he said thickly.

'Never!' Defiantly she glared into his eyes. It was the worst thing she could have done, for their silvery brilliance seemed to pierce her, shattering her anger and leaving only treacherous desire, so that when he placed his mouth on hers again she accepted it without fight.

Why not? she asked herself, allowing its sinuous movements to arouse her. This is all I'll ever have of him.

Aware of her surrender, he let go her hands, and she clasped them around his neck and caressed the dark hair curving into his nape, then ran her fingertips across his shoulders and down his spine.

Jason's touch grew gentler, his tongue delicate as he teased the soft inner skin of her mouth, then withdrew it and slid it down the side of her neck to the creamy curve of her breasts.

Her dress was no barrier to his eager hands, and her nipples were soon bare to his ardent gaze, stiffening into peaks as he suckled first one and then the other.

She ached for him, longed for him, yearned for fulfilment. Yet even as she trembled on the brink of total surrender, self-esteem held her back. She had never given herself to any man, and to do so with one who so easily doubted her moral integrity would cheapen an act that should be based on mutual love.

Taking advantage of his relaxation, she slid from under him in one adroit movement, pulling up the bodice of her dress as she hurried to the door.

'Get out!' she spat. 'Get out before I call the police and accuse you of trying to rape me!'

'An idle threat, sweetheart,' he taunted, rising slowly. His hair was dishevelled, his skin flushed, adding to his vibrant sensuality and making her regret that she would never know him as a lover.

'If you change your mind,' he went on, sauntering past her into the hall, 'give me a call.'

'Only when we can weekend on Mars!' she flashed.

Grinning wolfishly, Jason went down the path to his car, leaving Lorraine to close the front door on him and all the hopes she had ever fostered for their future.

CHAPTER TWELVE

THE PHOTOGRAPHS Bud Weston had taken of Lorraine for *Vogue* appeared in the August issue, and within hours of the magazine hitting the bookstands the Belinda Pearce Agency received five bookings for her.

Lorraine was thrilled, and for the first time optimistic about a successful career in England.

'Next you should go to Stanway Hall,' Sally said that evening, when she and Denis came to dinner. 'If you see for yourself that the children are happy, you won't pine so much for them.'

'I can't face meeting Lord Stanway.'

'You'll have to sooner or later,' Denis interjected.

'I'd rather it was later.' Lorraine rose to clear the plates. 'Incidentally, don't you want to sell this house and put the money into the children's trust fund?'

'No. Property prices are increasing and it's better to keep the house.'

'Then I'll pay a proper commercial rent.'

'Edward wouldn't have wanted you to.'

'*I* want to.'

Her tone brooked no argument, and he nodded.

In the weeks that followed, her career and bank balance grew apace. But on the personal level Jason still occupied all her thoughts, and she continually remembered his duplicity and wondered whether he had meant any of the loving things he had said to her.

Some hope, she chided herself in her gloomiest moments. If he'd cared in the slightest he'd have realised

she could never had had a one-night stand with the
Larry Pethcos of this world. Or with anyone else, for
that matter!

She found herself telling James the whole sorry
story one hot, sunny day when he took her for a drive
and she discovered they were heading for Brighton—
the last place she wanted to go to again!

Alert to her sudden anxiety, he probed as to the
reason for it, and she satisfied his curiosity over a
picnic lunch on the Sussex Downs.

Hearing how Jason had reacted to the photographs
of Larry leaving her room, James came out unexpectedly on Jason's side, arguing that love or wounded
ego could make a mockery of one's intelligence, and
that Jason should be excused on these grounds.

'*You* wouldn't have doubted me,' Lorraine argued.

'I'd have been damn jealous,' he admitted, 'though
I hope I'd have had the sense to hear your side of the
story before condemning you.'

'Unlike Jason,' she snorted.

'I've known you longer,' James reasoned. 'Anyway,
I might well have reacted as he did.'

'Never!'

'Thanks for the note of confidence!' James idly
played with her fingers. 'A little while ago you said
you were in love with someone who wasn't free. It
wouldn't be Jason, by any chance?'

Red-cheeked, Lorraine looked away. 'I—er—I'm
afraid it is.'

'Stupid of me not to have guessed. Is there no possibility of——'

'No,' she interrupted. 'It's over. Finished. Not that
it ever really began. It was all an act on his side.'

James said nothing for several moments, though his words, when he finally spoke, came as no surprise to her.

'I'm not asking you to marry me this instant, Lorraine. But I want you to think about it. I'll be here a year and a half, and perhaps you'll get Jason out of your system by then.'

It would have been easy to give him hope, but she liked him too much to do so.

'I could never marry you, James. You'll always have a special place in my heart, but what I feel for you isn't enough for marriage.'

He put his fingers on her lips. 'Forget what I said. If friendship's all you can offer, I'll settle for that.'

His ready acceptance of the situation didn't fool her for a moment. 'I don't believe you.'

'What a thing to say to a man who's just stuffed you with caviare and pâté and the best French cheese!'

Her smile was tremulous. 'Darling James, you've been an absolute haven for me. But I've no intention of commandeering your spare time. You must take out other girls.'

'Yes, ma'am.' He refilled her champagne glass. 'Incidentally, Jason's in the news.'

Her hand shook, and though she was aware that James noticed he pretended to ignore it. 'His new book?' she managed to say.

'No. Hang on while I get the Sunday paper from the car.' He came back with it, riffling through the pages till he could show her the one he wanted.

Carefully composing her features, Lorraine read the paragraph he indicated.

' ''Jason Fletcher, whose books are full of exciting venues, is off to an exciting venue himself with the lovely Erica Robson. *He* says it's to film a documentary in Kenya, *she* says it's to research his next book. Either way, they agree they're going together.'''

'They make a fine pair,' she said laconically. 'They've known each other for years, and their families are friends.'

James made no comment, and Lorraine kept up a flow of small talk, insisting, when they finally arrived home, that he come in for coffee.

'I feel guilty as hell for showing you that article,' he blurted out. 'But I wanted you to know that you were wasting your life carrying a torch for him.'

'Sweet of you,' she said and, as he coloured, added instantly, 'I'm not being sarcastic, James. I mean it. You made me face an unpleasant truth all over again, and it was good for me.'

'I wish to hell you never had to set eyes on him again.'

'When I do, I'll probably wonder what I saw in him in the first place!'

'I'll drink to that!' James raised his cup of coffee and so did she.

More than ever determined not to occupy James's time, Lorraine started dating other men, and was soon so busy juggling her time between modelling and would-be suitors that Belinda Pearce warned her to stop burning the candle at both ends.

'You're beginning to look haggard,' she reprimanded. 'And the camera will pick it up. I'm aware that it's tempting to be wined and dined, my dear, but you're in a profession that demands you be in tip-top condition.'

'You make me sound like a dog being groomed for Crufts!' she laughed.

'I couldn't have put it better myself!'

Taking Mrs Pearce's words to heart, Lorraine spent more time at home, and surprisingly discovered she no longer found it depressing to be alone. So much so that one weekend—after she had refused dates with two perfectly eligible males—her old desire to paint surfaced, and she produced a highly satisfactory sea-scape by Sunday midnight!

Who said there wasn't life after Jason? she asked herself jocularly. A year from now she'd have trouble remembering who he was—provided she didn't bump into him when visiting the children.

This thought reminded her to find out when she could go and see them, and she was still vacillating about it when Margaret rang to say they were coming up to the dentist on Friday morning, and Lady Stanway had suggested they stay overnight with their aunt.

Delighted, Lorraine prepared their room, then spent the following day hurrying round the shops buying Paul and Jilly's favourite food.

It was wonderful having them back with her, and within half an hour it was as if they had never been away. Listening to their chatter, she realised that, though they missed her, they had settled down happily with their grandparents, and she faced the possibility that it might be in their interest for them to remain there.

In the afternoon she took them to the Zoo, and they spent a couple of hours wondering from the aquarium to the panda, the reptile house to the panda, the aviary to the panda!

'I could watch him for ever and ever!' Jilly exclaimed for the umpteenth time when Lorraine suggested they move on.

'Me too,' agreed a pale-faced girl of about twelve next to them.

A well-dressed man in his early forties walked up behind the girl and put his hands on her shoulders. 'Don't you think we should move on, Maria? There are many other animals to see.'

Maria shook her head and the man slanted a smile at Lorraine. 'You're having the same problem, I believe!'

He had a well-modulated voice with a slight accent, and after a moment's pause Lorraine guessed it to be Italian. He was only a few inches taller than herself, but his trim physique and upright carriage made him seem taller. His black hair was greying at the temples and brushed sleekly away from his olive-skinned face, and his features were melancholy until he smiled, when his dark eyes glowed with hidden fire. Not a handsome man, she decided, though a highly attractive one.

'Amazing the pull animals have over youngsters,' she said. 'When I was Jilly's age, I wanted to be a vet.'

'And did you become one?'

'I'm a model,' she laughed, stopping as she saw his eyes widen. 'I'm not a great advert for my profession at the moment,' she apologised, smoothing her hair and conscious she wasn't wearing a smidgen of make-up.

'If all women were as beautiful as you without cosmetics, I'd be out of business.'

'Oh, you're a make-up artist?'

He laughed. 'I'm Carlo Aldini.'

This time her 'oh!' was a yelp of embarrassment, for Aldini Cosmetics were among the most expensive and best in the world. Avoiding his eyes, she hastily told Paul and Jilly it was time to go.

'Do please be my guests for tea?' Mr Aldini suggested.

Lorraine hesitated, but Jilly decided for her, slipping her hand through Maria's, and tugging her forward.

'You look remarkably young to have a son of Paul's age,' the man said when they were seated in the Zoo tea-room.

In an undertone she explained about the car crash, adding that the children were now living with the Stanways.

'They're fortunate to have grandparents and an aunt who loves them,' he remarked. 'Since my wife's death, Maria has only me.'

'Has it been long?' Lorraine kept her voice low.

'Three years. Since then it's been a battle against loneliness for both of us.'

'I'd have thought you'd have masses of friends.'

'I have. But none that can make up for that one special woman.' He gave a rueful smile. 'So I've turned into a workaholic—my wife would have said *more* of a workaholic—and my business has grown even larger!'

'You built it up from scratch, didn't you?' Lorraine said.

'I'm flattered you're aware of it.'

'Don't be so modest. You're famous, Mr Aldini!'

'So famous that you clearly know all about me, which leaves me free to find out about *you*!'

Amused, she filled him in on her background, enjoying his obvious interest in her, and increasingly aware of his quiet attraction. Only when she spied Jilly giving a yawn did she decide it was time they left for home.

'Are you parked nearby?' Carlo Aldini enquired.

'We came by bus. It was easier than searching for a parking place.'

'Then please let me drive you home.'

Predictably his car, though a Rolls, was a conservative dark green. It went with the discreet designer clothes, the barely noticeable Piaget on his wrist. Lorraine would wager a pound to a dollar he was equally discreet in his personal life, and though he had said he didn't have 'that one special woman', she doubted he was entirely without female companionship.

She was convinced of this when he did not suggest seeing her again, and when he drove off—with Maria waving madly through the window—Lorraine was wryly amused. So much for her fatal charm!

Still, it had been an enjoyable meeting with an attractive and intelligent man, and should serve to remind her that the eligible male population didn't begin and end with Jason Fletcher!

One day she'd fall in love again and be happy. What was it her sister-in-law had once said? 'Expect happiness and eventually it will come to you.' Perhaps she'd take up embroidery and stitch that comment on a sampler to hang above her bed!

CHAPTER THIRTEEN

THE FOLLOWING week Lorraine was busy filming a commercial for Top Flight Travel. It necessitated her going to Mustique, Jamaica and Rio, and she returned to London on the Saturday, too exhausted to do anything except sleep away the weekend.

On Monday she was booked for a photo session and, still feeling the result of jet lag, cancelled a date she had made with a pursuing banker, in favour of an early night.

But ten-thirty still found her wide awake and restless, and deciding a warm bath might soothe her she was on the verge of stepping into one when the telephone rang.

'I hope I'm not calling too late?' Carlo Aldini said.

Hiding her surprise at hearing from him, Lorraine gave a soft laugh. 'I've been asleep for hours,' she joked.

'Then I apologise.'

'Please don't,' she said hurriedly, surprised he hadn't guessed she was teasing, and making a mental note of it. 'I rarely go to bed before midnight.'

'Me too. I've just flown in from Hawaii. I had to go there the day after I saw you—that's why I didn't call you before.'

'I see.' The knowledge was a fillip to her ego. 'How's Maria?'

'Fine. She was very taken with you—as I was. So much, in fact, that I wonder if you'd care to audition for this year's "Aldini Girl"?'

Lorraine's heart skipped a beat. What a boost to her career if she became the 'Aldini Girl'! 'I'd like that very much.'

'Good. Then shall we make an appointment for you here?'

Where was here? she wondered. If he suggested his home, she'd say 'no' and be done with it.

'Will my office at ten o'clock the day after tomorrow suit you?' he went on. 'We have our own studios here, and Lucien Sherwood will be working exclusively on the campaign.'

Wow! This was sounding better and better, for Lucien Sherwood was to photography what Mozart was to music.

'I'll be there on the dot,' she promised. 'Thank you for thinking of me.'

'I haven't stopped thinking of you since we met.' The very calm of Carlo Aldini's voice gave greater force to his comment, and she was searching for a reply when he spoke again. 'Until the day after tomorrow, Lorraine. I know you don't like the bother of parking, so I'll send a car for you.'

'Oh, no, that isn't necessary. I can take a cab.' All she needed was to arrive for an audition at Aldini's in the boss's car! The tongues would wag faster than a puppy's tail!

At five minutes to the appointed hour, Lorraine presented herself at the ten-storey block in Knightsbridge, flagship of Aldini Cosmetics. The ground floor was given over to a shop lavishly displaying all the company's products amid designer dresses, bags and belts.

She took the lift to the top floor as instructed, and found herself in a large reception area exotic with orchids and palm trees and the latest high-tech in Italian desks and chairs. But this was as nothing to the opulent office of Carlo Aldini himself, which seemed to be an acre of thick black carpeting filled with Art Deco settees and armchairs in silver-grey birch and azure suede, the colours epitomising the pots and phials of the Aldini cosmetic range.

The man himself was as quietly sombre as Lorraine remembered, as he rose from behind a large, curving glass-topped desk to greet her. His olive-skinned face broke into a smile, and intuitively she knew her appearance met with his approval. But then, why shouldn't it, when she had taken such care choosing a black linen suit that skimmed her tall, slender body and heightened the blonde of her honey-coloured hair?

'You look delightful,' he greeted her, leading her to a settee and sitting beside her.

She eased her hand away from his, uncomfortably aware that he had held it slightly longer than necessary, and hoping he wasn't going to be another Larry Pethco. Though the Italian was the acme of breeding and sophistication—which could never be said of Larry—men were still men when sexual appetite reared its head.

'I'm pleased you gave me the chance to audition for the "Aldini Girl",' she said matter-of-factly. 'It was very kind of you.'

'Kindness doesn't enter into it. You are the type I am looking for—I knew it the instant I saw you. But whether or not you are chosen is a matter for the board of directors.'

Considerably chastened, Lorraine's spirits plunged, then rose again. Hell! She was doing well at modelling and wouldn't starve if she didn't land this highly prized plum!

'It's time you met Lucien,' Carlo Aldini went on, glancing at his watch. 'You're booked for a ten-fifteen session with him.'

'Where must I go?'

'The end of the corridor, so you'll make it in time!' He brought her to her feet with him.

This time she noted that he was quick to drop his hand away from her elbow, and also careful to keep his distance when he accompanied her down the corridor.

Outside the studio he stopped. 'I don't know how long you'll be with Lucien, but if you're free to have lunch with me...'

'I've another appointment,' she lied, reluctant to have him think she was available.

'Dinner one evening, perhaps?'

'Fine.' Turning, she entered the studio.

It held none of the expected clutter. The various-coloured rolls of paper used as backdrops were stored at ceiling height and rolled and unrolled electronically, and dozens of arcs and spots were ranged like sentries against one wall.

The various costumes she was asked to don hung tidily from a rail in a beautifully equipped dressing-room, which came complete with bathroom, hair-dryer, and a range of Aldini cosmetics.

Lucien Sherwood was wonderful to work with. Unlike most fashion and beauty photographers, he didn't shoot fast frame after frame, keeping up a continuous flow of—'Wonderful! Marvellous! Lick your lips, angel. Make it sexier,' and other more erotic comments used to stroke a model's ego and encourage her to give her all to the camera lens. Instead he was as silent and composed as if he were photographing the Queen, and only when the session was over did he relax.

'I'm not usually as quiet as this,' he apologised, 'but Carlo wants this year's "Aldini Girl" to be aloof and untouchable. Hence my getting you in the mood!' He gave a puckish grin. 'Ten more sessions like this and I'll forget how to smile!'

'Is that the number of girls you're auditioning?' she asked.

'Treble that, Miss Ellis. I've already done twenty.'

So put that in your pipe and smoke it, she warned herself. Carlo Aldini might have put her forward as an applicant, but he wouldn't allow his liking for her to rule his business head if the board of directors turned her down. Which was the way she wanted it, she assured herself. If she won the job on merit alone, she'd owe him no favours.

'I hope you've no objection to working with animals?' the photographer asked.

'Dogs or cats?'

'Lions and giraffes, actually! We'll be doing some work in Kenya.'

Where Jason was! Her heart leapt. She might even bump into him! But that was silly. Kenya was vast, and they could both be there for years without ever crossing paths.

'I once did a commercial with a lion,' she said aloud. 'Apart from losing two pounds in nervous perspiration, I was fine.'

'I'll make a note of that,' he grinned, and saw her out.

For the remainder of the week Lorraine was on tenterhooks, and, every time the postman came or the telephone rang, her heart beat a wild tattoo.

'If the Aldini job doesn't come to anything,' Belinda Pearce said to her two weeks later when she came in to collect money due to her, 'you can always reconsider signing that Rowena contract. Larry Pethco's still keen on having you.'

'I bet!' Lorraine sniffed.

'Take a few judo lessons and accept the job!'

'Not even if Larry doubled my fee.'

Belinda Pearce pulled a face, and as Lorraine returned home she wondered if she were being foolish. After all, forewarned was forearmed, except that Larry had eight arms when he chose! She chuckled and dismissed him, suddenly confident she had done the right thing.

There was a message from James on her answerphone, saying he would like to take her to dinner and would she call him if she were free. She decided not to be, aware that it was in his best interest, though by eight-thirty she regretted turning him down, and she curled up on the settee with a bar of chocolate and watched television.

At nine the telephone rang and she snatched it up. If it was James trying his luck again, he'd hit the jackpot! But it was Carlo. Her scalp prickled.

'Hello, "Aldini Girl",' he said.

Lorraine was speechless.

'Are you still there?' he asked.

'I—just about. I—would you mind repeating what you called me?'

'"Aldini Girl". We all found you stupendous.'

'I can't believe it!'

'Have dinner with me tomorrow and I'll convince you.'

'I'd love that,' she told him.

They dined at Mossiman's, one of London's newest and best restaurants, and she learned that the board's decision to engage her had been unanimous, and that her earnings for the year would be twice what she had expected. Career discussion over, Carlo went on to tell her a great deal about himself and his marriage, which had been a happy one. Encouraged by his openness, she unburdened her own problems, careful to make no mention of her emotional attachment to Jason. By the time Carlo left her she was completely at ease with him and had accepted his invitation to the opera for Saturday.

This time he made no reference to his wife, and their conversation was strictly of the present and his plans for the future. Only business ones, she noted, for he was careful to say nothing personal. Yet as they sat together in their box, perfumed by the flowers he had ordered for it, she was conscious of him watching her in the darkness; and though he made no move to touch her, she sensed his desire to do so.

During the next month they went out several times, but as her departure for Africa drew nearer her days became frenetic, filled with visits to dress designers, hairdressers and beauticians, so that by evening all she wanted was a hot bath and bed.

Inevitably she dreamt one night of Jason, and, waking at six, she padded down to the kitchen to make herself a hot drink. Sipping it, she allowed the memory of him to flood her mind. There was no pain! She was over him! It was such a wonderful thought that she let herself visualise his tanned face and blue-black hair, his sardonic eyes and sensuous mouth. Yes, he was a handsome devil, but he meant nothing to her.

Refilling her cup in celebration, she switched on the Breakfast Show, debating whether it was too early to ring Sally—who knew how she'd felt about Jason— and tell her the good news. She was actually dialling the number when Erica Robson appeared on the TV screen.

Lorraine set down the receiver. What was Erica doing on a programme like this?

'How does it feel to be voted best publicist in publishing?' asked the interviewer, his question giving Lorraine her answer.

'It isn't difficult to be the best when you have the best novelists to promote,' Erica said modestly, looking unusually soft and feminine in pink silk which did everything it was supposed to for her colouring and doll-like figure.

'Who's your favourite novelist?' the interviewer continued.

'They're all my favourites, though I've a soft spot for Jason Fletcher because I've known him since I was a little girl.'

'Do I sense romance?'

'That would be telling!'

The interviewer's smile was feral. 'But you *are* rejoining him in Kenya, I believe?'

'To help publicise the documentary he's making.'

Lorraine heard no more, jealousy engulfing her, engulfing all sound. As if anyone in their right mind would believe such a story! Jason had only to pick up the telephone and every newspaper or magazine reporter would fall over themselves to interview and promote him. So why take Erica with him?

Angrily she switched off the set and paced the floor. So much for her belief that she was over him! She pounded her side with mortification, and repeated her childish habit of speaking her thoughts aloud—which in this instance turned the air blue!

At last, drained by temper, she sat down and allowed herself the honesty of assessing where she was. At a crossroads, she knew, one leading to the past and unhappy memories, one to a future that, with determination, she might make a happy one.

There was no contest as to the route to take, nor the man with whom to take it.

Goodbye, Jason. Hello, Carlo.

CHAPTER FOURTEEN

THE DRY African bush stretched as far as the eye could see as the minibus carrying Lorraine, Lucien and the film crew made its way along the dusty brown roadways of the wildlife sanctuary.

They had already glimpsed a herd of zebra, and would have completely missed two giraffes, whose yellow and brown patterned bodies blended with the yellow and brown trees they were busy denuding of leaves, had Tambu—their driver—not pointed them out.

'Extraordinary!' exclaimed Denise, the make-up artist. 'We can take a lesson from the animal world when it comes to camouflage.'

'I'm waiting to see a lion,' said Lorraine.

'You see, you see,' beamed Tambu, his large white teeth like polished marble in his ebony-black face.

True to his word, a mile further on they came upon an enormous tawny lion basking with his lioness in the short grass by the roadside. Their appetites were obviously sated, for they blinked lazily at the mini-bus, disregarding it and the remains of a buffalo carcass next to them.

'Poor buffalo!' Lorraine shivered.

'No be sorry for him, missy. Buffalo kill plenty people if have chance. You not leave bus ever.'

'You'll have to prise me out of it,' she assured him, and Lucien laughed.

It was mid-afternoon when, exhausted from the bumpy ride, they arrived at the safari lodge where they were to spend their first night—a comfortable hotel of cedarwood and stone.

'I'll meet you all in the bar at seven,' Lucien announced. 'I'm going to have a sleep.'

'I'm for a swim,' Anton the hair-stylist said, a statement with which everyone else concurred, arranging to meet at the pool when they had unpacked.

None of them were booked in the main lodge itself, but in independent *rondavels*—circular, stone-built cabins with thatched roofs—each set in its own little plot of grass where one could sunbathe. They were furnished ethnically, with bed and wardrobe of local wood, and brightly coloured, hand-woven rugs and gaily patterned curtains.

As she stepped inside hers, Lorraine's eyes darted swiftly around for strange creepy-crawlies, in particular spiders. The mere thought of them brought her out in goose-bumps! Cautiously she wandered the floor, opening drawers and the wardrobe before relaxing. Then, just to be on the safe side, she took out a spray from her holdall and used it liberally before sinking on to the bed.

Above her the mosquito net drifted in the breeze from the overhead fan. The gauzy fabric reminded her of a bridal veil, though its functional use was not to be ignored.

'A few bites on your face, Lorraine,' Lucien had warned her, 'and we'll lose a couple of days' shooting and thousands of pounds!'

Remembering this, she lowered the net over the bed after she had unpacked, and, with a loose cotton dress over her bikini, meandered along the path—bordered by exotic flowers and bushes—to a surprisingly large pool near the main lodge.

'Watch you don't get sunburnt,' Anton advised as she settled on a sunbed beside him. 'I don't relish working on a sizzled face!'

'Damn! That means no tan!'

With a scathing look, he planted her straw hat squarely on her face. 'Definitely no tan.'

Pushing her sunbed under a large umbrella, Lorraine went into the pool. Then, resisting the urge to sit on the edge to dry, she returned to the shade. Luckily it was as warm out of the sun as in, and the heat unwound her.

'Anyone fancy watching the animals drink at the waterhole?' one of Lucien's two assistants asked.

Everyone agreed that it was a great idea, and returned to their rooms to don more suitable clothing; a long-sleeved cotton dress in Lorraine's case, for at sunset mosquitoes bit more ferociously.

Tambu was waiting to escort them, and they walked as quietly as possible to the hide, a cabin covered with leaves, where they could peep through windows yet remain out of sight.

In the gathering dusk they waited, expectation high, and found it fully justified when, in ones and twos, animals usually seen by them only in zoos appeared before them in their freedom: waterhogs guzzling, the quiet elegance of deer drinking peacefully beside a group of giraffe. Graceful when roaming the grassland, the latter were amusingly awkward when bending down to drink, their long knobbly legs splayed outward to bring their long necks within reach of the water.

Lorraine could have sat in the hide for hours, but the rest of the party were more interested in sundowners, and, not wishing to be thought unfriendly, she was obliged to join them.

The other guests at the lodge were predominantly German and Swedish, and as she sat on the terrace, drink in hand, only the vast expanse of starry sky and whirr of crickets and cicadas told her she was in Africa.

'Make the most of tonight,' Lucien advised, joining her as they all trooped in to dinner. 'From tomorrow on I'll be working your butt off!'

She knew he wasn't joking, and went with him to the buffet to fill her plate. Since the children had gone, her appetite had gone too, and she had to force herself to eat, which she did now more than ever, conscious that it was important to have sufficient protein and nutrients in a hot climate.

She was forcing down some coconut pie when she was called to the telephone. It had to be Carlo, she thought, crossing the wood-floored dining-room, and knew a sense of pleasure as well as disquiet to find she was right.

'I wanted to make sure you'd arrived safely and settled down,' he said, sounding so close, he could have been beside her.

'Everything's fine,' she replied. 'It was kind of you to call.'

'You think it only kindness? I'm too old to play games, Lorraine. You know how I feel about you.'

'Yes, well . . .'

'We won't talk of it now. It is better face to face.'

'Carlo, I——'

'No, my dear, no discussion. Sleep well, and don't let Lucien slavedrive you.'

'You'll have to be the one to tell him,' she said drily.

'I already have! So return to your dinner, my dear.'

The line went dead and she returned to her table, trying to look carefree but inwardly disturbed by Carlo's declaration. She would be a fool to turn him down, yet she was by no means sure she was ready for another relationship.

For the next three days they all worked non-stop. It wasn't the posing that tired Lorraine so much as the frequent changes of clothes, as well as the exotic hair-styles and make-up she was obliged to wear in the exhausting heat.

'I can't believe any woman buying Aldini cosmetics wants to look like this,' she grumbled on the third afternoon, when she had donned a jewel-trimmed safari suit, and had her eyelids painted green and purple to match the green and purple Anton had sprayed on her hair.

'These photographs aren't for make-up,' Lucien called, his camera whirring away. 'It's for "Safari", your Carlo's new scent.'

Lorraine was instantly aware of 'your Carlo' and, from the glances exchanged between the crew, knew they'd noticed it too. But she was an old hand at this game of gossip and completely ignored it.

'I hope it doesn't mean you'll be photographing *me* with a lion?'

'No, it doesn't.' Lucien's winged eyebrows rose higher. 'But it's a thought!'

'Like hell!' she exclaimed, and they both laughed.

By the end of the week the bulk of the shooting was over, and Lucien visibly slackened. So did

Lorraine, who found she was enjoying herself more than she had anticipated. But then she hadn't expected that being on safari would be so civilised. Even her *rondavel*—sparsely furnished though it was—had a homely look about it now it was scattered with her belongings.

About to change for dinner, she realised she had time for a nap before showering, and, slipping off her slacks and T-shirt, she lay back on the pillows. The overhead fan was on and the faint whirr was soothing. She had left the curtains undrawn, and though she couldn't see the bright blue sky she enjoyed the brilliant green foliage and grass, and the scarlet and pink hibiscus. Drifting into sleep, she was awakened by the sound of a radio—loud and then swiftly muted. But it was enough to make her look at her watch. A good thing too, for she had barely half an hour to be ready.

Padding into the stone-floored shower-room, she placed her towel on a stool and stepped on to the slatted wood floor of the shower cubicle. Turning on the water and adjusting the temperature, she washed the dust and grime of the day from her body, then wound her towel sarong-fashion around her before squeezing the water from her long hair. Tilting her head to let the tresses fall back, she found herself staring directly at a gigantic, hairy black spider!

With an ear-splitting scream she leapt from the bathroom into the bedroom, and was half out of the door when she collided with the broad-shouldered figure of a man rushing in to see what was wrong. The breath was knocked from her body and she would have fallen if strong arms hadn't supported her.

'Th-thank you,' she stammered, still shivering with horror, then grew more horrified as she found herself staring up into astonished silver-grey eyes. Jason's!

For several seconds they regarded each other, with Jason the first to gain control.

'What the hell were you screaming for?' he demanded tersely.

'A tarantula!' she shuddered. 'In the shower!'

Dropping his hands from her, he stalked across the bathroom and stepped inside.

Lorraine waited close to the outer door, gripping her towel firmly in place. Almost at once Jason emerged.

'I sent it down the loo,' he said laconically. 'It won't bother you again. And it wasn't a tarantula, by the way!'

'Oh, lord,' she muttered, 'I can't wait to leave here. Until this minute I was enjoying myself, but——'

'I'm sorry I affect you like this.'

'You?' Her temper rose as she saw his amused expression. 'You don't affect me in the least. I meant that—that thing in there!'

'A baby spider?' he mocked. 'It was more scared of *you*.' His eyes roamed over her. 'You needn't hold on to your towel for such dear life. I'm not going to ravage you.'

Instantly Lorraine was aware of the skimpiness of her bath towel and the curves of her body all too evident beneath it. She searched for something cutting to say, but her brain appeared to have turned to cotton wool. Luckily her legs were still functioning, and she moved away from the door.

'Thanks for the rescue,' she managed to mutter. 'You've done your good deed for the day.'

'The spider wouldn't agree!'

She shuddered again. 'I've a phobia about them.'

'Many women have!'

'Erica too?' Lorraine couldn't refrain from asking.

'Erica too.'

'I believe she's here with you?' How casually she managed to say this. No one would guess she was shaking with rage at the very thought.

'She flew back to London a few days ago.'

Jason leaned negligently against the wall. The African sun had deepened his tan and his hair had grown longer, which served to increase the virile masculinity of him. It emanated from him like a laser beam, drawing her towards him. Stop it! she ordered herself, and half turned away from him.

'How is it *you're* here?' he asked. 'Or should I say with whom?'

'Five men!' she spat at him, and would have laughed at his frozen astonishment if she hadn't been so furious. 'I'm working for Aldini Cosmetics,' she concluded.

The winging eyebrows rose higher. 'Don't tell me you're the new "Aldini Girl"?'

'How clever of you to guess!'

'It's my business to keep up with the news,' he said sardonically. 'I never can tell what may be useful for a story. If——'

The tap of heels on the path cut him short, and a second later Denise came in view.

'Oops!' she exclaimed, eyeing the tall, bronzed man with admiration. 'Sorry if I'm intruding, Lorraine.'

'An ex-neighbour of mine from London,' Lorraine said casually. 'He rescued me from a spider.'

Denise gave Jason a wide smile, provocatively tossing back her beautifully tinted red hair. 'Haven't I seen you somewhere before? On television, perhaps?'

'I doubt it,' drawled Jason. 'I avoid the box whenever possible.'

'Then you *are* a celebrity.'

'I'm a writer.' He went to move away.

'You're talking to the great Jason Fletcher,' Lorraine said deliberately, and Denise's round blue eyes grew rounder.

'Wow! My favourite author! I thought your last book was the greatest!'

'Kind of you to say so.' He drew back a step and Lorraine hid her amusement, aware that, anxious as he was to go, he didn't want to upset his 'public'!

'Are you a model too?' he asked with a faint smile.

'I'm make-up artist for all "Aldini Girl" adverts.'

'An important job,' he said politely, then glanced at Lorraine. 'You've made the big time.'

'Luckily,' she replied coolly. 'I've a great incentive to be successful.'

Instantly it was as if a shutter came down over his face. The mouth set tight and the lids lowered.

'Are you here on holiday, Mr Fletcher?' Denise put in.

'I'm doing a documentary, and this is my base for the rest of the week.'

'Then I hope we'll see you around.'

He smiled wordlessly and retreated down the path.

'What luck to have had a neighbour like that!' Denise exclaimed. 'How about asking him to join us for dinner?'

'I'd rather not.' Lorraine retreated into the bathroom, still glancing fearfully about her. 'I won't be long,' she called. 'I'll join you on the terrace in ten minutes.'

Only when she was alone did the full impact of Jason's presence at the lodge impinge on her, and she was all fingers and thumbs as she dressed. 'Tried to dress' would be more apt, she thought wryly as trembling fingers smeared her lipstick, fumbled the zip of her lilac voile shirtwaister, and set her high-heeled sandals skittering across the floor as she reached down for them.

But eventually she was ready and, a mass of nerves, joined the crew at their usual table on the terrace, slipping into the vacant chair always left for her beside Lucien.

'If you see any more spiders, call *me*,' he chuckled.

'Denise told you?' She sipped the Margarita ordered for her and glanced at the flame-haired make-up artist. Naturally Denise would tell everyone. Jason was a celebrity and it was a coup to meet him. Funny to think she herself rued the very day she had!

With an effort she joined in the conversation, but had no real awareness of what she was saying or hearing, her mind debating if she had judged Jason too harshly. Viewing the situation from the detachment of passing time, she saw how hard it would have been for him not to do as his uncle had suggested, and, though he had inveigled himself into her life, she had been equally responsible for their impassioned lovemaking. Which meant she could hardly accuse him of trying to seduce her!

No, what had hurt most was his reaction to those damned photos of Larry leaving her room at the Metropole!

Would he have believed in her innocence if she had tried to explain herself, instead of responding to his contempt with fury?

Sipping her drink, she thought of the fire in his eyes as he had looked at her a short while ago, and knew that, regardless of what he had said, he still desired her. But was it only desire, or something deeper? Perhaps he was fighting his love for her as she was fighting hers for him.

But where did Erica fit in? In the answer to that lay the key to everything, and she was considering what to do when Lucien suggested they go in to dinner.

She was halfway through her meal when Jason came into the dining-room. Busy though it was, his arrival did not go undetected, though it had less to do with his fame as an author—Lorraine doubted he was recognised—than his aura of vibrant masculinity.

Casually he glanced around, and, whether by accident or design, met her eye. As their glances held she knew exactly what she had to do, and gave him a tremulous smile. Her heart raced as his face softened, white teeth gleaming as he gave her an answering one that held none of his previous mockery.

A waiter came to his side and indicated a table overlooking the terrace, but with a shake of his head Jason started walking purposefully in Lorraine's direction.

Her fingers trembled and she set down her fork, trying not think, just hoping, hoping.

Suddenly she was encircled from behind by two strong arms.

Startled, she tiled her head back and saw Carlo beaming down at her. As she went to greet him, his

head lowered to cover her mouth with his. The first
time he had kissed her, and it had to be in front of
Jason!

Quickly she pulled her mouth away. But not quickly
enough, for Jason had already seen it and was heading
for a table as far from her as possible!

Lorraine wanted to scream with frustration. It was
incredible! First, Larry, then James, and now Carlo;
and each time Jason had misread the situation.

'Don't be angry with me for kissing you,' whispered Carlo, misinterpreting her expression. 'But I've
missed you so much, I couldn't keep away.'

She mumbled incoherently, glad that the welcoming greetings from around the table helped mask
her misery. A space was made for him, naturally
beside her, and as she made an effort to resume eating,
she caught Denise's sly grin. And no wonder, for Carlo
was a circumspect man, and to have kissed her so
publicly was tantamount to a declaration.

Desperately she tried to catch Jason's eye as they
finally returned to the terrace, but he resolutely refused to look her way.

'Lucien says the shooting's going very well, and that
he's ahead of schedule,' Carlo was saying.

'By two days,' Lorraine agreed, forcing a smile to
her lips.

'Then he won't mind if I steal you away. I thought
we'd spend a few days at Treetops.'

Lorraine tensed, aware that her friendship with
Carlo had reached crunch point, and dismayed that
it had done so here, where their every move would be
noted.

'It's a long drive to Treetops,' she said lightly. 'I'd
rather stay put.'

'There's our macho man,' Denise's voice came across the table. 'If you've ever considered an Aldini Man, Carlo, there he is!'

Carlo followed the girl's gaze to Jason at the top of the terrace steps. In the golden glow of the lanterns his white drill suit against his copper tan gave him a god-like appearance, in no way diminished by the aloof manner with which he surveyed the scene before sauntering to a table overlooking the pool.

'He's far too handsome to sit by himself,' Denise announced, and, jumping to her feet, undulated over to him.

Either the girl's thick as a plank, Lorraine thought irritably, or she's being deliberately mischievous. She waited for Jason to give Denise her come-uppance, astonished when he allowed himself to be led to their table. With a flourish Denise introduced him to everyone, ensuring he knew that the man sitting on Lorraine's left was Carlo Aldini, though her triumph was negated when Jason nonchalantly left her side and took the vacant chair on Lorraine's right.

'Jason was once Lorraine's neighbour,' Denise said brightly, hiding her chagrin.

'You never told me you had such a famous neighbour,' teased Carlo.

'I wasn't really aware of Jason's fame.' Lorraine spoke with an effort. 'I simply regarded him as a good Samaritan.'

'That's just what I can do with,' Denise interjected, batting her lashes at him. 'If you're thinking of moving, there's an empty apartment next to mine!'

'Sorry,' Jason said with a faint smile. 'I've returned to my old apartment at the Albany.'

'Much more high-class than Balham!' Denise sighed so dramatically that everyone laughed, after which the conversation became general.

Lorraine was too edgy to join in, and wondered how soon she could politely retire to her room. Yet it would be rude to leave Carlo, and she knew she had to sit out the evening.

'Is Aldini the new man in your life?' Jason's low voice in her ear made her turn sharply towards him. Carlo had moved his chair slightly to talk to Denise and Lucien, leaving the two of them momentarily isolated.

'I work for him, as you very well know,' she said tonelessly.

'Seems to me he wants you for his personal Aldini girl.' The sardonic smile was back on Jason's mouth as his eyes roamed her face and the shadowed cleavage between her breasts.

'He's a kind friend, nothing more. And I'm not in love with him.'

'Since when was love important to you?'

'Don't judge others by your own standards!' she bit out.

'Touché,' he sneered. 'I despise you, but have to admit you're extremely desirable.' Once again his eyes dropped to the soft swell of her breasts. 'We can still make it together, Lorraine. It could be memorable.'

Rage swamped her, blanking out everything around her, though she was aware of Jason pushing back his chair, murmuring goodnight and walking away.

Only then did Lorraine gain control of herself, and, muttering that mosquitoes were making a meal of her ankles and she needed to apply more repellent, she hurried after him.

He was striding ahead of her, but she didn't call to him until she was out of earshot of the terrace.

He stopped and turned, waiting for her to reach him.

'We—we have to talk, Jason,' she blurted out. 'All these misunderstandings are crazy. There's nothing between Carlo and me—I swear it.'

'As there was nothing between you and Pethco, or you and James whatever-his-name-is? I may make a living out of fantasy, but I sure as hell don't believe in it!'

'Do you enjoy thinking the worst of me?'

'I don't enjoy anything about you. My duty to my uncle obliged me to know you, but as the children are where they belong, I can put you out my life.'

'I meant nothing to you?'

'Not nothing. As I said back there on the terrace, I find you very beddable. But if you're angling for anything lasting, forget it.' With a careless gesture he touched his hand to her lips, then turned on his heel and walked on, his leisurely pace as much an insult as his words.

Lorraine stood where she was, a frozen statue in the warm African night. Her attempt to talk rationally to Jason had ended with an even wider breach between them, and she finally accepted that she had lost him forever. Except one couldn't lose what one had never had.

'Lorraine, what is it?'

Numbly she saw Carlo coming towards her, his slim body moving with the refined grace of a puma.

'I was chatting to Jason,' she said, uncertain whether Carlo had seen her with him.

'I saw.' Carlo walked noiselessly beside her as she continued towards her *rondavel*. 'Denise's suggestion was an excellent one, come to think of it.'

'Suggestion?' she queried.

'Having an "Aldini Man". He'd be ideal—not only handsome, but famous.'

Lorraine stared at Carlo as if he'd gone out of his mind. Did he honestly think Jason would agree to promote aftershave or men's make-up? This was the best laugh of the evening! 'You'd more easily persuade Prince Charles,' she retorted.

'Don't be so sure. He could name his price—almost. The two of you would be sensational. Your colouring would make an excellent foil for his.'

'Jason's the last man I'd want to work with,' Lorraine insisted.

'Such vehemence!' Carlo chided, bending his head towards her. 'Why do you dislike him so when he was such a wonderful neighbour?'

She thought fast. 'I don't dislike him. It's just that I don't enjoy his sarcastic outlook on life.'

'Oh. For a moment back there on the terrace I had a suspicion you felt more than neighbourly towards him.'

'Oh, Carlo, *please*!' Her tortured emotions could take no more this evening.

'I'm sorry, my dear, but I love you so much, I can't bear you looking at another man.'

Lorraine closed her eyes. This was worse than she had anticipated. A showdown with Carlo had been inevitable, but she had hoped that when it came it wouldn't be emotional.

'Am I rushing you?' he asked.

'I—I'm not ready for love,' she stammered. 'There's so much I still want to do with my life.'

'You can do it with me.'

'No, I'm not the girl for you, Carlo. Find someone else.'

His olive-skinned face was serious. 'I'm asking you to marry me, Lorraine. I'm not looking for an affair.'

Oh, heavens! she thought despairingly. The wrong man, the wrong time, the wrong everything. She couldn't cope.

'Am I too old for you?' he went on. 'Is that why you——?'

'No, no. I've never given a thought to your age.'

'Then I'll go on hoping.'

'I wish you wouldn't,' she said earnestly. 'I don't want you on my conscience.'

Carlo half smiled. 'I'm a grown man, my dear. I can take care of myself.'

The round hut came in sight, and never had it been more welcome. Lorraine quickened her pace, and had her key in her hand by the time they reached the door.

'Will my remaining at the lodge worry you?' Carlo asked quietly.

She considered the question, then knew she owed it to him to be finally blunt. 'It will worry and sadden me. One can't love to order, and realising how you feel about me...'

'Love can beget love, Lorraine. Marry me and I'll prove it.'

She shook her head, then asked the question she had to. 'Will seeing me in your advertisements upset you, Carlo? If it will, I'm willing to tear up our contract.'

'I wouldn't dream of it. Your business arrangements with my company have nothing to do with our—with our friendship.' He paused. 'I'll wait another day before flying home, or it will look strange.'

'Of course.' She hesitated. 'Thank you, Carlo. I wish I . . .'

Unable to go on, she went inside and closed the door, wishing, as she had done many times before, that she could love to order.

CHAPTER FIFTEEN

LORRAINE returned to England on a dank autumn day that held no signs of the mists and mellow fruitfulness of September. Hard to believe that only hours before she had been basking under the blue skies and heat of Kenya.

Quickly she settled down to her normal routine, glad there were no lulls between assignments, and that she was kept busy rushing from one photographer's studio to another.

At the end of the week Carlo called to say the contact prints were ready and would she care to come in and see them.

Though nervous of meeting him again, she went. But, maintaining his word that their personal relationship had nothing to do with their business one, he was friendly but impersonal, leaving it to Lucien to show Lorraine the photographs splayed out on the desk.

'They're sensational!' she enthused.

'I only photographed what was there,' he replied.

'You're both wonderful!' joked Carlo. 'And I was right about your being the best "Aldini Girl" we've had. How do you feel about giving us your exclusive services for the next three years at least? We'll make it extremely attractive financially.'

This was what Belinda Pearce had anticipated, and Lorraine was delighted. 'Fine with me, but Mrs Pearce must make the decision.'

'I'm sure we'll work out an arrangement,' Carlo replied, and opened a bottle of champagne to celebrate.

Lorraine was relieved when he didn't suggest lunch, though the look in his eyes as she left told her he still loved her and had not given up hope. Was she foolish, keeping him at arm's length? she asked herself as she drove home.

She was still musing on this as she opened the front door and heard the telephone. She dashed to answer it, fear rising when the woman at the other end introduced herself as Elizabeth Stanway.

'The children?' Lorraine asked instantly.

'Paul's fine. But Jilly had a bronchial chill while you were away, and hasn't picked up as well as she should. We think she's pining for you, and if you could spare the time to——'

'I'm never too busy to visit Paul and Jilly,' Lorraine cut in. 'I'll be with you soon after four.'

'That's wonderful. Would you—er—perhaps you'd like to stay for a few days?'

'If you think it will help her,' Lorraine said stiltedly.

'I'm sure it will.'

An hour later she was zooming along the motorway, on the back seat of her car a hastily packed case containing her simplest dresses. She'd give Lord Stanway no chance to make another unpleasant comment about her overdressing!

She was tense with nerves by the time she turned in at the massive iron gates and drove along the winding drive to the stately Tudor pile that was Stanway Hall. Parking in front of the black and white timbered mansion, she realised why the Stanways wanted their grandchildren to be brought up here.

As she stepped from the car, a rotund little man in butler's livery came out through the massive oak door to collect her case, and as she entered the high-ceilinged hall, its size minimised by the vast rectangular table and arch-backed Tudor chairs in the centre, a door on her left opened and Lord and Lady Stanway came forward to greet her.

The man seemed less gaunt and his manner less offensive than she remembered; his wife pinker than on the day of the funeral. They were both in tweeds, his a well-worn suit, hers a softly gathered skirt topped by a lavender silk blouse that lent warmth to her silver-grey hair.

'We both appreciate you coming,' the woman murmured.

Lorraine gave a stiff smile and half glanced at Lord Stanway, who met her eyes without evasion.

'Jilly will be delighted,' he said stiltedly. 'She's been watching the clock since we told her you were on your way.'

'I'll take you to her,' Lady Stanway put in, and led the way through a stone archway and along a thickly carpeted corridor. 'The nursery suite's on the second floor,' the woman went on, 'but we've turned the garden room into their playroom—so we can pop in and see them more easily.'

The room was large and cheerful, though the sight of Jilly's waxen face came as a shock.

'You're here, you're here!' the little girl cried, dancing up and down with delight. 'I thought you'd gone away forever!'

'I'd never do that,' Lorraine said fiercely, hugging the thin body close. 'But I've been working out of the country, and didn't know you hadn't been well.'

'Are you going to live here with me?'

'For a few days.'

'I want you to be here forever.'

Jilly's lips trembled ominously and Lorraine said quickly, 'I'd love to see your toys. I bet you've got masses of new ones.'

The simple ruse did the trick, and Jilly was immediately engrossed showing off her treasures.

'Gran'pa and Gran'ma gave me a doll's house last week, and Paul got a big 'lectric train.' She ran over to her grandmother and clambered on to her lap.

Amazingly, Lorraine felt no jealousy, nor when Jilly jumped down and put her hand in Lord Stanway's large one, asking him to show Lorraine the tree-house he had had built for them in the garden.

'You'd best not go outdoors yet,' he said gently. 'Your aunt's staying here for a while and you can show it to her in a day or two.'

At that moment Margaret wheeled in the tea trolley, and they all tucked in to scones and cream. No need to wonder if Jilly was happy here, Lorraine knew, for she didn't stop chattering, and her grandparents were in no way disturbed by her high spirits.

'I'm sure you'd like to see your room,' Lady Stanway said when tea was over.

'I'll show her, I'll show her!' Jilly cried. 'Come on, Lorri.'

The room Lorraine had been given was on the first floor, and overlooked a lake whose calm surface was ruffled by half a dozen gliding swans.

'I don't know which is lovelier,' she exclaimed, looking round at the delicate Regency furniture, 'the room or the view.'

'That's what Anne always said.' Lady Stanway's voice was thick with emotion. 'It was hers.'

Lorraine's surprise was evident, and the older woman touched her arm.

'Paul and Jilly have spoken so much about you, it's as if I've known you for years; I'm sure Anne would have wanted you to use her room.'

Poignantly Lorraine looked around, gently touching the Lalique bottles and bowls on the dressing-table. Jilly skipped over to sit on the chaise-longue by the window to watch the swans, and the two women exchanged smiles.

'She's so like her mother,' Lady Stanway murmured. 'If only...' Her voice died away, and it was a moment before she resumed. 'There's nothing worse than living with regrets; wishing one could turn back the clock and handle things differently. But unfortunately one can't, and the only way to make amends is not to make the same mistakes again.'

'You don't have to explain yourself to me, Lady Stanway.'

'But I want to. It's important that you understand. You're the children's aunt and I don't want there to be any estrangement between us. The main reason we opposed Anne's marriage was that we felt she was too young and we wanted her to wait. She'd been a hole-in-the-heart baby, and because of it we tended to cosset her.'

'How would you have felt if my brother had been rich?'

A flush stained Lady Stanway's cheeks, but she met Lorraine's eyes unflinchingly. 'Differently, of course. You have to admit he was in no position to support her.'

'I can't,' Lorraine said staunchly. 'Edward couldn't keep her the way *you* wanted, but she was never short of the things that mattered. Their home overflowed with love. I understand your misgivings,' she went on in a choked voice, 'but to cut her out of your life...not even to relent when Paul was born and she wrote to you...'

'We tried,' Lady Stanway asserted, 'but she didn't want to see us.'

'I don't believe it!'

'It's true. We were in Australia when Paul was born, but the moment we returned and found her letter we went to see her. By then she and the baby had gone on tour with your brother, and the landlady didn't know where to contact them. She said that the moment Anne returned she'd tell her we'd called, and we left a letter for her saying we loved her and were longing to meet our grandson.' Lady Stanway's hands twisted together convulsively. 'We waited and waited, but never heard a word from her and—well, we—we thought your brother had forbidden her to meet us.'

'Edward would never have done that.'

'It was the only explanation we could think of for Anne changing her mind.'

Lorraine was still incredulous. She didn't doubt that Lady Stanway spoke the truth, yet she knew Anne would never have turned away from her parents.

'You say you gave the letter to their landlady? Perhaps she forgot to pass it on.'

'I'm sure not.' Lady Stanway drew a tremulous breath. 'She even made a joke about it. Said her surname was Brain, and a guarantee that she'd remember to hand over our letter.'

'Brain? Oh, heavens!' Lorraine sank on to the dressing-table stool. 'Anne never received your letter. The house burned down while they were on tour, and Mrs Brain died in the fire. Edward wrote to me about it. He was terribly upset.'

Lady Stanway went corpse-pale, and her mouth moved wordlessly.

'Anne never knew you wanted to contact her,' Lorraine whispered. 'If she had, nothing could have kept her away from you.'

'If we'd only realised...' The shaky voice broke on a sob. 'I must tell Henry. Lord knows how he'll bear it, he loved her so.'

'Why are you crying, Gran'ma?' Jilly piped in.

'I'm not,' came the muffled reply. 'I've a—I've a speck of dust in my eye.'

Satisfied, Jilly beckoned Lorraine to her side. 'Come and see where Jason's going to live. It's called the Dower House.'

Anxious to give Lady Stanway an opportunity to collect herself, Lorraine joined Jilly at the window, and when she looked round a moment later the woman had gone.

'Jason's in Africa,' Jilly babbled on. 'He sent us a photograph of an elephant and he——'

'Would you like to help me unpack?' Lorraine cut in, unwilling to hear anything about him.

Jilly complied, and by the time they reached the nursery Paul was home from school and overjoyed to see her.

Lorraine played with them until it was time for their baths and when she offered to read them a bedtime story afterwards they giggled and said they were having dinner with her as a treat.

'Gran'pa said we can stay up till you go into the drawing-room for coffee,' they stated.

'That will be very late indeed,' Lorraine said solemnly.

'If you don't have coffee we can keep up for ever, and ever!' Jilly cried delightedly.

Laughing, Lorraine went to her room to change, and was brushing her hair when the butler came to tell her that Lord Stanway wished to talk to her in the library when she was ready.

Dreading the meeting, she stepped into the book-lined room. Gone was the upright man she had encountered a few hours before, in his place a broken one, his face as ashen as it had been on the day of his daughter's funeral.

'My wife told me Anne never received our letter,' he said thickly. 'And it's a sorrow I'll have to bear for the rest of my life.'

'I'm so sorry,' Lorraine murmured.

'We missed so much,' he went on as if he hadn't heard. 'All the years Anne had left . . . Paul as a baby, then Jilly . . .'

Unable to continue, he bowed his head, and Lorraine, aching for his loss, searched for words to comfort him.

'I'm sure Anne knows. Your love for her children will be your link with her.'

'I hope so,' he whispered. 'It's the only thing that can make my guilt bearable.' His head remained bowed and, feeling intrusive in the face of such sorrow, Lorraine backed to the door.

'Please don't go,' he said, unexpectedly looking up. 'I can't make amends to our son-in-law, but if you can find it in your heart to forgive a stupidly arrogant man for the way he's behaved to you, then——'

'It's past,' Lorraine intervened. 'We must put it behind us.'

Lord Stanway's eyes met hers. 'For the moment,' he said huskily. 'But later there's much that has to be said. Meanwhile . . .' Rising, he came towards her and held out a hand.

Mutely she clasped it, then together they went to meet Lady Stanway and the children.

Inevitably dinner was a constrained affair, though both the Stanways did their best to hide their grief. But, the moment Paul and Jilly were in bed, Lorraine retired too, sensing that her host and hostess had much to talk over between themselves.

Next day, Lady Stanway said she was welcome to remain as long as she wished, and because Lorraine was concerned about Jilly's peakiness she contacted her agency and asked them not to make any bookings for her until she called them again.

'We can't anyway,' Mrs Pearce said. 'Aldini's have bought your exclusive services, and Lucien's just informed me that your next session with them is in ten days.'

Lorraine was astonished that things had been settled so fast, and even more astonished to hear the vast sum she was to receive. Had this news occurred a few days before, she would instantly have instructed Denis to fight for the children's return, but now she couldn't do it. They had settled in well here, were happy living in a magnificent home with grandparents who plainly adored them. Besides, what she had learned last night had changed her whole attitude to Anne's parents.

She said as much to Lady Stanway later that morning, and was so warmed by the woman's pleasure that she realised how much she had missed not having a mother herself during her teenage years.

As the days passed a great affection developed between Lorraine and the Stanways, though it wasn't until the Saturday that her hostess referred to the private detective they had engaged to watch her.

'We were desperate to have the children,' she confessed, 'and our lawyer suggested it.'

'Then why did you use Jason?' This was a question that had long puzzled Lorraine.

'Originally to act as detective, but he disconcerted us by suddenly saying he considered you suitable to remain their guardian.' Colour heightened the lined cheeks. 'I'm afraid we took his comment with a large pinch of salt—Jason's always had an eye for a pretty face—and decided to hire an outside man.'

'I was livid with you,' Lorraine confessed. 'But even more with Jason for the double game he played with me.'

'I can appreciate that. But when he knew you, he was sincere in wanting to help you. And, of course, now that we know you ourselves, my husband and I can understand why. We love having you with us, Lorraine, and we'd like you to look on our home as yours.'

Lorraine was touched to tears. 'It's very kind of you, Lady Stanway, and——'

'Elizabeth, please. And my husband would like you to call him Henry. This "Lord and Lady Stanway" bit sounds so stuffy.'

'I can't imagine myself calling your husband Henry!'

'You'll get used to it after the first few times,' Elizabeth Stanway chuckled, and by the end of the evening was proved right.

It was only as Lorraine rose to go to bed that Henry Stanway said what had obviously been on his mind since he had broken down in front of her on the day of her arrival.

'Elizabeth and I appreciate how much you love the children and—and we want to share them with you.'

'I'm so glad.' Lorraine blinked rapidly. 'You've made me feel so at home here, I'll visit whenever I can.'

'That wasn't what we meant.' A gnarled hand smoothed back hair that, though grey, was still thick and strong. 'We want you to have the children during the school holidays.'

Lorraine was staggered, yet, much as she wished to accept the offer, she knew it wasn't sensible to keep taking Paul and Jilly from Stanway Hall, though she wouldn't say no to the occasional vacation with them.

'If ever you change your mind . . .' Henry Stanway said.

'I won't. Anne would want them to grow up here.'

'Then don't forget this is your home too.'

She nodded, though she knew that if Jason intended making the Dower House his home she'd have to curtail her visits. She'd only be able to bear seeing him as long as he was single, but once he was married it would be unthinkable.

CHAPTER SIXTEEN

'YOU really must see the Dower House before you go back to London,' said Elizabeth on the Thursday morning, when Lorraine announced that she had to return to work. 'Jason was in the middle of redecorating it when he went to Kenya, and we suspect he's thinking of getting married.'

Lorraine was careful to school her expression. 'He and Erica are very friendly, aren't they?'

'Yes. They've known each other forever. She dotes on him, of course, but I'm not sure he reciprocates it. Still, as Henry says, he must be doing the house up for a reason. Let me show you round it.'

'Next time I come down,' Lorraine said hastily.

'We have time today. You're not leaving till after lunch, are you?'

Since she wasn't, Lorraine had no alternative but to give in, and stolidly walked across the lawns with her hostess.

The Dower House was set some two hundred yards from the Hall, and unwillingly she found herself falling in love with the sloping roof, the lopsided chimneys and old stone walls covered with Virginia creeper.

'It's much bigger inside than it looks,' Elizabeth said, unlocking the oak door and preceding Lorraine into a small octagonal hall carpeted in honey-gold.

'What a pretty colour!' Lorraine exclaimed.

'Jason had it especially woven. He plans to do the house in shades of cream and gold and rust.'

Slowly they wandered the downstairs rooms. The dining-room and living-room were complete, and Lorraine admired the happy marriage of antique and modern furniture.

'There used to be a wonderful chaise-longue in front of the window,' Elizabeth explained, 'but Jason said he preferred sofas and gave it to us. It's in your room now.'

'It's very attractive,' Lorraine lied, suddenly recalling that she'd once told Jason how much she disliked chaise-longues. It seemed she'd convinced him of their discomfort, she thought wryly.

Elizabeth led the way upstairs, where four bedrooms, each with its own bathroom, had been furnished with a lavish disregard for money.

'Wait till you see the main bedroom,' she said, opening its door with a flourish.

Lorraine smothered a gasp as she took in the glowing peachy walls and deeper-coloured carpeting: old-fashioned carriage lanterns on the walls either side of it.

'He scoured the country for those.' Elizabeth indicated the lamps. 'He wouldn't settle for anything else.'

Lorraine was scared to believe what her brain was telling her, yet she had to; Jason had furnished this room, this whole house, for *her*!

Remembering their last devastating meeting in Kenya, it didn't make sense. Yet he had discarded the chaise-longue, taken trouble finding these lanterns and decorated the entire house in her favourite colours. Hope burgeoned within her. Jason must have realised he had misjudged her, and no longer saw her as a girl who played fast and loose with men's emotions.

But then he had gone to Kenya and seen the way Carlo had greeted her!

'What's happening to the house now?' she asked.

'Nothing. Mrs Perrin, his interior decorator, called us the other day to say she hasn't heard from him for weeks. So he's either too busy to concentrate on it or—as Henry says—may have decided to remain a bachelor!'

Neither! Lorraine longed to shout. He's simply doubting me all over again. Yet it wasn't fair to involve Elizabeth in her problems. She had to sort them out herself.

Should she fly out to Jason, or wait till he returned? One thing held her back—his sardonic attitude towards her in Kenya, even before Carlo's arrival. But hang on! Thinking back on the scene in her room after he had rescued her from the spider, hadn't she noticed a change in his behaviour towards her, as if he was debating what to say to her? Then Denise had appeared on the scene, and their next meeting had been when Carlo had pulled her into his arms to kiss her!

Lorraine's spirits soared. She'd go to Jason tomorrow, even if it meant flying to Kenya.

'Good heavens, it's nearly lunchtime!' Elizabeth broke into her thoughts, and Lorraine hastily composed herself and returned with her to the Hall.

She was too excited to eat, and was wondering whether she should, after all, give Elizabeth and Henry some inkling of her feelings for Jason, when the butler brought in the entrée and announced, 'Miss Erica was on the telephone a moment ago, Lady

Stanway. But when she heard you were at lunch, she asked me to tell you that Mr Jason is arriving from Kenya this afternoon, and that she's meeting him at the airport and bringing him directly here.'

'Why's he flying back?' Henry Stanway asked his wife. 'Last time he spoke to me he said he still has another month's filming.'

'It could be something to do with his book, dear.'

'Or else he's missing Erica,' Henry grunted.

'You could be right.'

Lorraine's hopes, earlier so bright, were utterly dimmed. Had Jason returned to see herself he wouldn't have asked Erica to meet him, and the fact that he had, and was bringing the girl here with him, meant he'd decided to make her his wife and wanted his aunt and uncle to be the first to know.

'Stay over to meet Jason, Lorraine,' Henry suggested. 'It would be nice to see you've forgiven him.'

'I have already,' she made herself say. 'But I'm afraid I've arranged to see someone this evening.'

Anxious to leave before Jason arrived, she had her case brought down to the car immediately lunch was over. She did not wish to make her departure a traumatic one for the children, so her goodbye to them was casual, and blowing them a kiss, she took her place behind the wheel. But, horror of horrors, the car wouldn't start!

'What a nuisance,' Elizabeth murmured. 'If the chauffeur were here, I'm sure he'd get it going. But he's in Leeds for his daughter's wedding.'

'Not to worry.' Lorraine hid her anxiety. 'I'll phone for a taxi to take me to the station.'

'Take my Volvo,' said Elizabeth. 'Then Charles will fix yours as soon as he's back, and drive it up to you and collect mine.'

The suggestion was so willingly made, Lorraine felt it ungracious to refuse. Her cases were transferred, goodbyes repeated, and she was finally on her way.

Only then did she force herself to think of Jason marrying Erica, and wondered how she'd find the strength to face them. A ghastly thought struck her. Elizabeth and Henry would expect her to attend the wedding! But that would be carrying face-saving too far. Come what might, she'd be out of the country when that dreaded day dawned.

Determinedly she turned on the radio full blast, and found herself wallowing in the melancholy strains of the *Pavane for a Dead Infanta*. How apt! Except that in the event of her own death there would be no one to mourn her so deeply, let alone compose a dance to her memory.

Never had the house in Hampstead seemed more unwelcoming than when Lorraine walked into it later that afternoon. In an effort to dispel the gloom, she turned on all the lights. Drat the expense! The 'Aldini Girl' could well afford it!

She had stopped at a supermarket on the way home for staple foods, and after unpacking them she showered and changed into a housecoat, then ate an omelette in front of a dreary sit-com on television.

She knew that a call to Carlo or James would bring them running, but she resolutely refused to take advantage of them.

Nine o'clock came and went, and she wandered restlessly from room to room. It was fine having a fabulous contract, but too many days of idleness would drive her crazy.

She heard a car drive slowly down the cul-de-sac. Its engine had a familiar sound, and peering through the window she was startled to find it was hers. The chauffeur must have cut his weekend short. How sweet of him to drive it up tonight. Picking up the keys of the Volvo from the hall table, she flung open the front door.

'Hi, Charles,' she called. 'Care for a cup of tea before you drive back?'

The car door opened and a narrow-hipped, wide-shouldered figure unfurled itself.

Lorraine fell back. She was hallucinating! But it was no hallucination that walked towards her, but a flesh and blood man with bronzed skin and a smile that set her pulses racing.

'Make it coffee,' he said.

'C-coffee?' she stammered.

'Or has the sight of me strained your hospitality?'

'Of course not.' She stepped aside for him to enter, breathing in the scent of him as he sauntered past her. 'It was kind of you to return my car,' she said, hurrying into the kitchen. 'You shouldn't have bothered.'

'I wanted to see you anyway.'

She desperately longed to know why, but determined not to ask.

'I gather you've been visiting my aunt and uncle?' he went on.

'Yes. I found them charming.'

'And vice versa.'

'Thank you.'

'You're welcome,' he said politely.

Not sure how to continue this banal conversation, Lorraine reached for the percolator.

'I don't suppose you have any cheese and crackers?' he asked.

She spun round. 'Yes, as it so happens. I shopped on my way home.'

'Anything interesting?'

She stared at him, noting for the first time the lines of weariness on his face, and that his skin, though tanned, had a greyness she hadn't seen before. 'Are you hungry?' she asked carefully.

'Starving.'

'I thought you were dining at the Hall?'

'I'd intended to. But when I found you gone, I had a quick drink and hared up here.'

'How did you realise I'd be there?' she asked, refusing to read anything meaningful into his explanation.

'I called you here a few times over the past few days, and finally contacted your agency. They told me.' He paused, then said abruptly, 'Hence my deciding to go there.'

'To see *me*?' she asked bluntly, trying to forget Erica had met him at the airport.

'Yes,' he stated, then took a chair by the table. 'Even a boiled egg would be welcome,' he said faintly. 'I was in no mood to eat on the plane, and I haven't had a thing since heaven knows when!'

Hastily Lorraine heated some soup and laid the table, then, while he wolfed it down, set a couple of eggs to boil and made toast. Watching him, she found it hard to believe he was actually sitting in her kitchen, large as life, and enigmatic as ever.

'Why *are* you here, Jason?' she repeated. Her nerves were giving way and she was afraid that if she didn't get him out of the house soon she'd disgrace herself by bursting into tears.

'I told you—to talk to you.'

'What for?'

He swallowed the last of his toast, dabbed a napkin to his mouth and leaned back in the chair. 'To apologise.'

'For what? You accused me of so many things.'

'One only,' he said quietly, 'with three different men. I don't know how you feel about Carlo Aldini— if you've decided you care for him, I can't say I'd blame you—but I sure as hell know I was wrong over that Larry Pethco business, regardless of those bloody photographs!'

'He was definitely in my room,' she said. 'Why are you suddenly so certain nothing happened, when for months you believed it did?'

'Because for months I was crazy with jealousy. It's never happened to me before. I never cared enough for any woman to give a damn how she felt about me. But with you it was different, and when I saw those photos, I lost my sanity.'

'And now you've regained it?'

'Through long nights of hot thoughts and cold showers,' he admitted wryly, and, pushing back his chair, came towards her. But he changed his mind half-way and turned towards the living-room. 'It's more comfortable there,' he said abruptly. 'I've had a hectic forty-eight hours tying things up so I'd be able to return home for a week, and I'm dead on my feet.'

Lorraine motioned him to go ahead of her, and waited until he had sunk on the sofa before taking the armchair opposite.

'It was really a question of coming to grips with my jealousy or living without you,' he continued. 'And that I couldn't face.'

'So you're willing to overlook my being an amoral woman?'

'You're no more amoral than Jilly!' he snorted. 'My problem was that I was too cynical to credit that any girl could be as innocent as you professed. Dammit, Lorraine, when I accused you of leading Pethco on, why didn't you deny it?'

'You didn't give me the opportunity. The minute you saw me you accused me of being a——'

'OK,' Jason cut in. 'But I rushed back that evening ready to hear your side of the story, and found you in another man's arms!'

'James's,' she explained. 'My brother's best friend, and a dear one of mine.'

'You could have told me.'

'You stormed off, remember?'

His sigh was a reluctant agreement. 'I behaved like a bear with a sore head. But when I bumped into you at Madame Tussauds, I nearly pulled you into my arms and said to hell with every man in your life, I loved you.'

'You could have fooled me!'

'I came to you that evening,' he reminded her, 'and what did I hear through the window? Some millionaire proclaiming that he adored you—a sentiment you appeared to endorse!'

Lorraine burst out laughing.

'What's funny about it?' Jason demanded, looking so strained that she knew he was by no means sure where her affections lay.

'You were wrong again, Jason. It was James. I was helping him rehearse the first instalment of his television series.'

Jason let out a long, deeply felt sigh. 'You mean I was listening to a *play*?' At her nod, he ran a hand across his face. 'Why didn't you say so?'

'Because I was angry too. I couldn't forget you'd moved next door to spy on me.'

'You told me you'd known all along who I was. You even said that was why you pretended to care for me.'

'I was lying,' she admitted. 'I never guessed who you were, and only said it to save my pride.'

'Within a week of knowing you, I was hating myself for what I was doing,' Jason said bluntly, weariness seemingly forgotten as he paced the floor. 'I tried to convince my uncle that the children should remain with you, and I was working out how to put the two of you together when he received those photos of Pethco.'

Jason stopped in front of her, and Lorraine tilted her head to look up at him. The greyness had left his face, replaced by a flush that spoke of tiredness as much as emotion. Though he was as well-dressed as ever, in well-cut trousers and a navy jacket, his hair was dishevelled and there was a faint sheen of sweat on his forehead. She ached to wipe it away, but refused to give in to the weakness.

'Where's Erica?' Lorraine was horrified to hear the question slip out.

'With her parents. She heard I was flying home and met me at the airport.'

'How?'

'By car, of course.'

'Not that, Jason,' Lorraine said crisply. 'I meant how did she know you were returning from Kenya?'

'She's friendly with the cameraman on my crew—I guess he told her. What does it matter, anyway? I want to talk about us, not Erica.'

'She matters very much,' Lorraine answered. 'She wants to marry you, as you damn well know.'

'Many women do,' Jason grinned, and in one swift movement leaned down and pulled Lorraine into his arms. 'Let's stop this talk and discuss feelings,' he said, his face inches from hers. 'I love you, Lorraine Ellis, and though you might be impressed by James's growing fame and Carlo Aldini's Italian charm, I believe that deep in your heart you care for me just that little bit more than you do for either of them.'

Lorraine tossed her head, her honey-gold hair falling free. 'You're wrong, I'm afraid, Jason.'

The flush faded from his skin and the greyness returned. 'Wrong?' he said huskily.

'Don't look like that.' She placed a hand to the side of his face. 'Please don't. What I meant is that I don't care for you a *little* bit more, but a hundred, a thousand, a million times more, and——'

The rest of her words were smothered by his mouth coming down hard upon hers as he dragged her close against him. There was no gentleness in his touch, nor did she want there to be. Gentleness would come later. Now they had their hunger to appease, their need for one another, the aching void existing within them for so long.

Deeply he drank of her, his tongue searching the soft depths of her mouth and draining the sweetness, his body hardening with passion. Pliant, she moulded herself to him, curve to curve, her legs entwining through his so she could more easily feel his arousal.

'Sweet Lorraine . . . I love you, want you.'

Urgently his hands moved over her body, caressing her breasts, her hips, her buttocks.

She answered him touch for touch, enjoying her sense of power as she felt him tremble. Their kisses deepened, growing wilder and wilder, until he suddenly pushed her away from him and stared at her with glazed eyes.

'While I can still think straight,' he said thickly, 'will you marry me?'

'Just try to escape!' she teased.

'Never!' Pulling her back into his arms, he sank down on the settee with her and they lay close in its comfortable depths.

'I need a shower,' he said a moment later.

'You need me.'

'That too.'

'Before or after?'

'Why not during?'

She blushed so brightly that even in the dim light of the lamps he saw it.

'Sweet Lorraine.' Gently he caressed her breasts. 'There are so many things I'll enjoy showing you. I hope you're a very slow learner.'

Surprised, she pulled back to meet his eyes. 'Why?'

'Because then I'll have the pleasure of showing you again and again!'

Laughing softly, they rose, and hand in hand went up to her bedroom.

Harlequin Presents®

Coming Next Month

Available in October wherever paperback books are sold, or through
Harlequin Reader Service:

In the U.S.
901 Fuhrmann Blvd.
P.O. Box 1397
Buffalo, N.Y. 14240-1397

In Canada
P.O. Box 603
Fort Erie, Ontario
L2A 5X3

From *New York Times* Bestselling author
Penny Jordan, a compelling novel of ruthless passion
that will mesmerize readers everywhere!

Penny Jordan

Silver

Real power, true power came from
Rothwell. And Charles vowed to have it,
the earldom and all that went with it.

Silver vowed to destroy Charles, just as surely and
uncaringly as he had destroyed her father; just as he had
intended to destroy her. She needed him to want her . . .
to desire her . . . until he'd do anything to have her.

But first she needed a tutor: a man who wanted no one.
He would help her bait the trap.

Played out on a glittering international stage,
Silver's story leads her from the luxurious comfort of
British aristocracy into the depths of adventure,
passion and danger.

AVAILABLE IN OCTOBER!

 HARLEQUIN

Take 4 bestselling love stories FREE
Plus get a FREE surprise gift!

PASSPORT TO ROMANCE
SWEEPSTAKES RULES

1. **HOW TO ENTER:** To enter, you must be the age of majority and complete the official entry form, or print your name, address, telephone number and age on a plain piece of paper and mail to: Passport to Romance, P.O. Box 9056, Buffalo, NY 14269-9056. No mechanically reproduced entries accepted.

2. All entries must be received by the CONTEST CLOSING DATE, DECEMBER 31, 1990 TO BE ELIGIBLE.

3. **THE PRIZES:** There will be ten (10) Grand Prizes awarded, each consisting of a choice of a trip for two people from the following list:
   i)   London, England (approximate retail value $5,050 U.S.)
   ii) England, Wales and Scotland (approximate retail value $6,400 U.S.)
   iii) Carribean Cruise (approximate retail value $7,300 U.S.)
   iv) Hawaii (approximate retail value $9,550 U.S.)
   v)   Greek Island Cruise in the Mediterranean (approximate retail value $12,250 U.S.)
   vi) France (approximate retail value $7,300 U.S.)

4. Any winner may choose to receive any trip or a cash alternative prize of $5,000.00 U.S. in lieu of the trip.

5. **GENERAL RULES:** Odds of winning depend on number of entries received.

6. A random draw will be made by Nielsen Promotion Services, an independent judging organization, on January 29, 1991, in Buffalo, NY, at 11:30 a.m. from all eligible entries received on or before the Contest Closing Date.

7. Any Canadian entrants who are selected must correctly answer a time-limited, mathematical skill-testing question in order to win.

8. Full contest rules may be obtained by sending a stamped, self-addressed envelope to: "Passport to Romance Rules Request", P.O. Box 9998, Saint John, New Brunswick, Canada E2L 4N4.

9. Quebec residents may submit any litigation respecting the conduct and awarding of a prize in this contest to the Régie des loteries et courses du Québec.

10. Payment of taxes other than air and hotel taxes is the sole responsibility of the winner.

11. Void where prohibited by law.

COUPON BOOKLET OFFER TERMS

To receive your Free travel-savings coupon booklets, complete the mail-in Offer Certificate on the preceeding page, including the necessary number of proofs-of-purchase, and mail to: Passport to Romance, P.O. Box 9057, Buffalo, NY 14269-9057. The coupon booklets include savings on travel-related products such as car rentals, hotels, cruises, flowers and restaurants. Some restrictions apply. The offer is available in the United States and Canada. Requests must be postmarked by January 25, 1991. Only proofs-of-purchase from specially marked "Passport to Romance" Harlequin® or Silhouette® books will be accepted. The offer certificate must accompany your request and may not be reproduced in any manner. Offer void where prohibited or restricted by law. LIMIT FOUR COUPON BOOKLETS PER NAME, FAMILY, GROUP, ORGANIZATION OR ADDRESS. Please allow up to 8 weeks after receipt of order for shipment. Enter quickly as quantities are limited. Unfulfilled mail-in offer requests will receive free Harlequin® or Silhouette® books (not previously available in retail stores), in quantities equal to the number of proofs-of-purchase required for Levels One to Four, as applicable.

PR-SWPS

OFFICIAL SWEEPSTAKES
ENTRY FORM

Complete and return this Entry Form immediately—the more Entry Forms you submit, the better your chances of winning!
- Entry Forms must be received by **December 31, 1990**
- A random draw will take place on **January 29, 1991**
- Trip must be taken by **December 31, 1991**

3-HP-1-SW

YES, I want to win a PASSPORT TO ROMANCE vacation for two! I understand the prize includes round-trip air fare, accommodation and a daily spending allowance.

Name_____

Address_____

City_____ State_____ Zip_____

Telephone Number_____ Age_____

Return entries to: **PASSPORT TO ROMANCE**, P.O. Box 9056, Buffalo, NY 14269-9056

© 1990 Harlequin Enterprises Limited

COUPON BOOKLET/OFFER CERTIFICATE

Item	LEVEL ONE Booklet 1	LEVEL TWO Booklet 1 & 2	LEVEL THREE Booklet 1, 2 & 3	LEVEL FOUR Booklet 1, 2, 3 & 4
Booklet 1 = $100+	$100+	$100+	$100+	$100+
Booklet 2 = $200+		$200+	$200+	$200+
Booklet 3 = $300+			$300+	$300+
Booklet 4 = $400+	____	____	____	$400+
Approximate Total Value of Savings	$100+	$300+	$600+	$1,000+
# of Proofs of Purchase Required	4	6	12	18
Check One	____	____	____	____

Name_____

Address_____

City_____ State_____ Zip_____

Return Offer Certificates to: **PASSPORT TO ROMANCE**, P.O. Box 9057, Buffalo, NY 14269-9057

Requests must be postmarked by **January 25, 1991**

- ✂ - - - -

 ONE PROOF OF PURCHASE   3-HP-1

To collect your free coupon booklet you must include the necessary number of proofs-of-purchase with a properly completed Offer Certificate   © 1990 Harlequin Enterprises Limited

See previous page for details